I0685482

For a Song

by

Lori Power

Gentle Surf, Book 3

For a Song

Cover Art by *RJ Morris*

The Wild Rose Press, Inc.
PO Box 708
Adams Basin, NY 14410-0708
Visit us at www.thewildrosepress.com

Publishing History
First Champagne Rose Edition, 2019
Print ISBN 978-1-5092-2509-5
Digital ISBN 978-1-5092-2510-1

Gentle Surf, Book 3
Published in the United States of America

Dedication

To my brother, Walter...
I still have the music mix you made for me.

Chapter One

Trip Vincent scrubbed his palms across his eyes. They itched and burned from the dry, recycled air. Under the pads of his fingers, the thick, worm-like scar that ran from the edge of his eyebrow along the contour of his eye to end at his cheekbone reminded him why he was there. The heat and odor of the mass of accumulated bodies crowding the courtroom caused acid to roll in his stomach.

He glanced behind him. Straight-backed, his sister, Evangeline, sat stoically in the front row. Shoulders squared, face pale but determined. The straight-edged nose and dimpled chin a mirror of his own. Despite her almost oppressive shyness, she had never wavered in her support, however much he had tried to shoo her away from the debacle.

When she caught his gaze, her eyes glistened in the fluorescent light. Still, she smiled. He tried and failed to return the gesture. Instead, he nodded and swiveled to face front.

"All stand, for the Right Honorable…"

Trip's bowels clenched, and his hands fell to the table top. All attention narrowed to focus on the rear of the dais. The remains of the bailiff's announcement were lost in the shuffle of people rising from the packed benches, their eagerness for the kill like a pheromone scent. An almost mystical hush descended, then a heavy cough echoed off the domed ceiling. Trip didn't need to hear the rest. He knew the routine well by this point of the trial.

A moment later, a stern-faced judge swept into the room from the alcove at the back of the raised stand. Cloaked in traditional legislative black robes and white cravat, he looked every inch the part. Wavy gray hair complemented the neat beard as he sped across the landing with a regal air. In the half second he took to regard the courtroom, the man's small, deep-set, penetrating gaze controlled without an utterance. Unquestioned authority permeated every pore. No nonsense would be tolerated.

Then he sat. His robes billowed like a cloud before settling around him while he shuffled some papers on his desk. Justice Moore's presence seemed to suck the oxygen from the room. A shifting of his gaze to the bailiff, followed by a nod, and everyone obediently resumed their seats.

Everyone except Trip Vincent and his lawyer.

Tremors rippled the length of Trip's legs, and he swore if he looked down, his knees would be knocking. Clenching his jaw, he suppressed the chatter of his teeth. Never had he been so frightened. His long fingers splayed across the surface of the polished wooden table while he forced his joints to lock. *Be a man.* A flutter twitched under his right eye, and he squeezed both shut. None of this mattered. His hands balled into fists. *All over soon.*

Whatever the verdict, the punishment would never bring his best friend back. To the marrow of his bones, he knew this to be the truth. No one cared that he hadn't been driving. They assumed, and in his grief, he hadn't corrected them. Trip opened his eyes to face the magistrate, willing himself to wake from the nightmare.

The judge signaled Trip's lawyer. "Be seated," he said. The crisp voice carried across the room. Each syllable struck Trip like a hammer in expectation.

Trip stared at Moore, whose prominent feature, a pronounced lower jaw, seemed to amplify every word. The trim goatee did little to soften the effect. Yet Trip remained grateful that today would mark the end of the debacle. Months of media frenzy, prosecution via the social mob, where no one seemed to care for the real story.

Except his family. And that was to be expected, wasn't it? He'd asked himself many times this last year, wavering between self-doubt and loathing. Yet he couldn't subject his grandparents to this media fiasco and had begged they stay away. For his sake, they'd agreed. To see them criticized for his choices and mistakes would have been too much.

Yes, he'd managed to keep family away, except his very stubborn twin. There were few things he could control at the present, and if he could shelter his family from exposure due to association, he would do all in his power to accomplish this. Though they didn't make even this task easy.

He'd been the brunt of bad jokes on late-night television. A media constant in prosecution entertainment while he tried to prepare for trial. The blame and shame hype had long since zapped Trip's zest for this life in the spotlight. Had he really craved the limelight as a youth? So much like his parents—his father a forgotten figure, never present and his mother still the starlet. He should have known better. Now, there seemed no safe harbor. No place to hide. Nowhere to escape. And he lacked the courage to even look.

His ears seemed deaf to the preamble of the judge. A buzzing, like bees gone mad, threatened his teetering sanity as he tried to concentrate.

In an unreality, he argued, pleaded, and fought the ghost of Kurt Davidson. Guilty, not guilty. In every debate, he won—and lost. Who had the keys that night? Who'd been in control? More importantly, who released the information that came as a total surprise to both his lawyer and the prosecution?

The name echoed in his brain, owned his memories, and stole his sleep. Kurt Nathanial Davidson. A name capitalized in every newspaper headline today. A name etched on a gravestone Trip had not had the audacity to see.

Trip ground his teeth and tried to distill the meaning of Justice Moore's words. To reengage in the here and now. To dig himself out of the void of black despair. A general gasp drew him back. Then his shoulders slumped, defeated before he even began. He hung his head. *What's the use*? Every day he relived the night his world tipped on its axis. Didn't anyone in this room realize he'd gladly welcome the cell if it would only allow him to escape the jail of his own memories—the iron smell of gushing blood, the gurgling sounds of the last rattled breaths, the vacant look that settled on the eyes alive no more?

He squirmed under the scrutiny and balanced on the edge of his chair. His foot bounced up and down as though a disembodied part. He couldn't help it. On his right, his lawyer, Cole Harvey, ever the cool cucumber, relaxed into position, an elbow hanging loosely from the back of his perch, fingers fanning. Every so often, his nose, bulbous as a turnip and the same purple hue to match, would flare—a sure sign Trip should pay attention. An accompaniment to the lawyer's lead, Trip would nod to the justice being meted out. Did that mean they were winning? How could they? Was Moore speaking English? Trip couldn't understand a word.

According to Harvey, this case warranted no jury. Trip's fate instead—his future—remained entirely in the hands of a judge—a man whom Trip referred to as "Jaws" whenever he recounted the events of the day to his sister during their daily debriefs.

With a flip of his wrist, Jaws focused on Trip. "Would the defendant, Travis Michael Vincent, please rise?"

Trip understood the motion and obeyed, forcing his body to unfold from the seat. His heart slammed against his ribs, and the urge to urinate almost overcame him. Then the pat from a heavily furred hand brought him back from the brink. "Ah, what?" Trip asked, turning blankly to face his lawyer.

A wide grin split the lawyer's face, revealing chemically altered, unnaturally white teeth, a stark contrast to the color of his nose. "We did it. You're all but free."

Trip shook his head. The rattle of bees intensified. "What…how?"

"Come on." Harvey's linebacker build towered over Trip's lithe frame. He tugged Trip by the elbow to thrust him forward. "Let's get out while we can. I've called for the car."

Spots blurred his vision. "How?" He shook his head, but the hallucination of Kurt remained fixed and fused behind his lids.

"How?" his lawyer parroted. Then Harvey turned his black, almost shark-like glower on Trip. The obsidian stare made his insides quake further. Trip couldn't comprehend any kind of good news. "Because I'm the best goddamned lawyer money can buy," he returned in a loud whisper next to Trip's ear. "And some secret admirer out there loves you enough to have found our golden bullet."

Trip had the sensation of swimming against the current. The pull of the ocean tugging him under. "But…"

An arm flung forward, Harvey parted the crowd. "Never mind," he said, tossing his head and forcing Trip to follow. "We'll go through the next steps in the car. We're near the finish line now."

The best money could buy. Where had Eva gone? Her seat was empty. Trip's focus fell to his business manager, Arnold Switzer, who sat unmoving in the front row. With a slight pivot of his head, he gazed in Trip's direction as though on autopilot when they scooted past. The corners of Arnold's lips lifted under the barrel moustache but fell far short of a smile. The crease between his eyes deepened, and his stare remained unfocused.

Trip ached to reach out to Arnold and ask him what this all meant. But Arnold's dark, lived-in face looked as mystified as Trip felt.

He shouldn't have forbidden his family from attending. Again, he searched for his twin. Perhaps a friendly face—someone who actually loved him—would help make sense out of all the confusion.

When had life become so chaotic? Certainly, long

before the trial.

Bailiffs held the heavy mahogany doors while they exited. Eva stood just outside waiting, her face warm. Camera flashes assaulted his vision. The flare rendered him momentarily blind. Still, he strode on, dimly following his lawyer through the gathering crowd, Arnold bringing up the rear.

On the periphery, jeers and catcalls resonated off the stylized stone walls. He opened his mouth to speak, but what could he say? He clamped his jaw together. No easy comeback popped into his vacuous mind. Easy had died. He couldn't muster enough anger at the insults to make an impression. Even the teenaged girl who threw broken pieces of his band's record at him, *Iron Clad's* Grammy-nominated fifth release, couldn't get a rise. Former fans ripped pictures of his face from magazines and tossed the crumpled pages at his feet while he walked on. And everywhere, smart phones recorded the scene to spread across the multitude of social channels. He continued to be a broadcast sensation. Now, for all the wrong reasons.

He thought he had long since given up paying attention to the armchair juries. They weren't saying anything he didn't already know. He, Trip Vincent, had killed the lifeblood of the band, their soul and future, *and* by the way, had gotten away with the evil deed. What they didn't know, didn't care to ask, was if this had been accomplished long before the crash that took Kurt's life.

Inaction, not a tragic car crash under the influence of drugs and alcohol, had taken Kurt. A ghost had sung the songs and answered mundane questions and accepted the awards and accolades. Only when Trip had decided to do something—anything—finally addressing the unaddressable, had his best friend's body joined his long-gone soul.

Suddenly, the red-tipped claws of an attacker pushed against his chest.

He teetered back a pace. Spread his stance while his hand groped for the wall to leverage his balance.

"Coward," Janet Davidson screamed directly in his face. Spittle sprayed across his nose.

Her eyes bulged, and foul, cigarette-laden breath gasped, wafting across his cheeks. A round face, near purple under a layer of cement-like foundation, sneered. Creases etched the contours, highlighting the age she tried desperately to hide. Her blood-shot eyes glowed under the incandescent lights. As though viewing the scene from an onlooker's perspective, Trip noted the eyeliner buildup in the corners.

"Community service! Who did you bribe?" Her talons tightened, and the pointed tips raked across his trunk. She leaned in and whispered, her breath hot and unpleasant, "How could you? You robbed him of any dignity he might have had."

Trip knew exactly what she referenced but had no idea where the information had come from. Relishing the pain for bringing him back to reality, Trip laid a gentle hand on her shoulder, remembering the smoothness of her bare skin, the softness of the girl she'd been, who awakened the man in him. How he ached to feel the love he'd once thought they shared. "Not me—"

"Bullshit," she shouted. "You're a coward. Kurt would be so ashamed."

A flurry of movement threw him back to the rough

stones of the wall. His hand dropped from Janet's shoulder, and he teetered again.

Then Eva's athletic, agile frame parted the crowd, revealing the path forward. She stood before him like a shield to the onslaught of war. "Get your hands off him," she said. She didn't need to yell. She exuded command. Trip had never noticed that about her before.

Janet glared but didn't budge. Retaining her grip on his shirt, she whirled to address the media, her other arm flung out in denunciation. The queen of the moment. Her theatrics, well documented in the past, had grown to epic proportions during the trial. "My brother's dead from this skiver druggy. My brother's dead, and he...he..." Janet released him then, and an accusatory finger shot up to his chin. "Gets community service—"

"Enough." Eva's voice, though not loud, drew attention easily. "Go home. Grieve."

Stubbed fingers with violently painted nails—reminiscent of oozing blood, sequins decorating the tips—pointed. "What do you know of grieving?" She shook her head. Sweat made the strands stick together in spikes. Then she postulated, "Either of you."

Eva reached for Janet's hand. "We all miss Kurt...like a brother—"

"Don't touch me. Don't you dare." Snake-like, Janet reacted swiftly and pushed Eva.

Heart pounding, Trip caught his sister prior to falling and lodged her behind him, guarding her from Janet's rage. He had thought he lost the ability—the strength, the need—to protect another. But he couldn't see his sister harassed. Not because of him.

Janet represented everything he loathed. She'd

altered the truth to influence the media—his fan base. Turned them against him, in her attempt to make Kurt a martyr. Her actions toward him were one thing, but he wouldn't allow her to touch or influence his family.

"No, Janet," he said, filled with a strength he'd thought he lost. "Do you hear me? No."

A squat security officer surged forward and took Janet by the elbow to maneuver her away from the mob.

His upper arm gripped by Harvey, Trip, too, pushed to the exit, losing sight of Eva.

The crowd surged with a cacophony of profanities to chorus Janet's outburst. Their swarming bodies surged against the guards lining the exit. The crush of the horde prevented Trip from even focusing on his shoes as he walked, let alone finding his sister. Looking everywhere but nowhere, he tried to avert his gaze from everyone.

Then a reflection in the glass doors caught his attention. A flash of something not a camera phone. He twisted, stumbling sideways through the mass. He scanned the sea of faces until he locked on another's. A pixie? Surely, a sprite. Small with spiked black hair, she stood to the edge of the room. Dark, with luminously large eyes, not seeming of this world, she dominated his attention. Perhaps the lack of movement, her calm in the sea of chaos, was what forced his notice.

Trip tried to stop the surge by his handlers, but he couldn't turn away. This small woman, dressed in plain, faded jeans and a white T-shirt, should never have been visible in this crowd, let alone gain notice. But she did. Even from the distance of the great entry hall, the dark pools of her gaze held him. In a moment filled with hatred and loathing, she gave him an impression of peace. Hope for a future. An emotion he had no right to sense.

Currents rushed across his skin, raising the hair. His breathing and heartbeat slowed to a temperate pace. Calm descended. More than sympathy etched her expression. A slight tilt of her head, the arched brows, conveyed an understanding. Reaching across the distance, eliminating the distraction of everyone else present, she delivered a message of hope.

"C'mon, Trip." His lawyer tugged his sleeve to keep him moving. "Let's get outta here. We'll work out the details later."

Trip turned to nod acknowledgement to the lawyer. Then the moment evaporated, and his heart faltered. Arching his neck, he scanned the crowd for the woman.

Gone. And with her his moment of grace. He swung around more fully, twisting against the pull, searching for her, grasping to *feel* again. Something— anything. But pandemonium surrounded him.

On his heels, Janet jerked against the restraint of the guard. "My brother's dead!" she screamed. "Do you hear me? Dead."

He laid his palm on his chest where Janet's hand had provided the only warmth his cold body felt in days. More than her words, the bruise would remind him.

He dropped his arm and stashed his hands in his pockets, then hung his head. He couldn't make contact. Not with Janet. Eva. Not anyone. Not anymore. He couldn't face his reflection in the glass doors.

"Murderer—"

A quiver racked him. His fists bunched, and he

ached to punch something. To be punished for his part. To split, to bleed. Something. Anything.

He didn't deserve freedom. He'd failed his friend.

"Shameful—" The heckles continued. The chants sliced into silence when the car door slammed against the protesters. Eggs splashed against the windows, the yolks a thick smudge. The wrong color, but reminiscent nonetheless of the texture of Kurt's blood when splattered over the windshield where the glass had impaled his chest.

Trip slumped down in the seat, removed his blazer, and pushed his shirt sleeves up to his elbows. His palms covered his eyes, and by habit, his fingers traced the thick scar.

Arnold slipped in on the other side of the car. His fingers beat out a tattoo on his knees. Trip expected the same silence he'd received from his manager these past two months. Instead, *Iron Clad's* administrator had miraculously, in the last few moments, seemed to shake off the black cloud, lifted his fingers from their drum solo, and patted Trip's knee in his old familial way. "We'll start again," the gruff voice barked from the round, brutish face.

Trip splayed his fingers wide to search Arnold's face for signs of lunacy. "Excuse me?" he croaked, clamping his jaw to ward off further words.

Only the smallest shadow of sorrow seemed to hang in Arnold's tawny gaze, the crease of his forehead lessened above the bushy brows when he smiled back. "You were always *meant* to be the lead singer. The industry is swamped with songs for the picking. A new songbook and we're off to the races, my boy. Capitalize on all of this frenzy. That's what Kurt would do. That's what we'll do. Your name is magic. Back on top in no time at all."

Was he serious? Just like that? Trip braced his fingers across the bridge of his nose. What was Arnold thinking? Kurt's ghost smiled sadly in Trip's mind. The image of his friend holding the syringe which shot him into a constant oblivion choked Trip's breath from his lungs.

Chapter Two

A melody, strange, yet familiar, whispered in her thoughts. Tangled with her misgivings.

Had she done the right thing? She had been exposed, spotted. That much she knew.

Aya Rose's thumb rubbed her temple, brushed her hair back. Didn't matter now. No time for regrets. She'd made the decision, found the information, and had Maury deliver. Trip walking out of the courthouse made the sacrifice worth the effort.

Scrambled vocals twisted with a tune just shy of awareness. Something new...but melancholy. She wished she had the time to write it down. Without pen and paper, the words and notes would continue to be elusive and out of reach. No time now, though in her mind, an acoustic guitar strummed, soft percussion accompanied the masculine words, amplified by the stillness of the night. Aya stopped, tilted her head, and glanced up to the stars above. If only she had her notebook at hand, she'd take the moment. But if it were worthwhile, it'd be there later. Maybe.

Such soulful eyes were out of place in such a strong face. She remembered how Trip had moved his sister behind him to protect her from that bitch, Davidson. He'd cut his hair for the trial. Typically, long, lanky locks drifted across his brow and obscured the slant of the almond-shaped eyes. She imagined the doctors had removed the hair when they repaired his face. Now, the trimmed, brown, artfully arranged mop revealed a vulnerability, in addition to the livid scar down the side of his face. But the little details hadn't escaped her notice. The vein across the plate of his brow, the smaller, purplish scars—on his cheek, along the ridge of his jaw. They, too, told the story even the trial didn't divulge.

Her hand covered her heart where the ache centered.

Not long ago, *Iron Clad's* manager, Arnold Switzer, had purchased her song. Now-deceased lead singer Kurt Davidson had sung it to the top of the charts and made it gold. Though she hadn't written the piece specifically for them, it was enough to make her curious about the band. Gazing at photographs, listening to his back-up, watching videos of him playing the piano, she'd wondered more specifically about Trip Vincent. How he'd accepted second fiddle when his voice resounded, pulling against the leash that held him back.

Then tragedy had struck, and against her own code, she persisted in keeping track. Knowing she'd threaten her own cover and place herself in danger, she attended the trial. She had to be there—in person—for the verdict. To hear with her own ears. To see with her own eyes. Not depend on secondhand accounts.

The musical phrases fluttered through the air, building the body of the ballad. Inspired, she closed her eyes and committed the music to memory.

She had to go. *Shevelis*, her grandmother would say in Russian, getting her off to school. *Shake a leg! Move it!*

Her family was not worth her thoughts. Aya

refocused and searched the surroundings. Dressed head to toe in black leather, she blended into the darkness of the early hours. She waited, breath shallow, still as a statue. On purpose, her shadow merged with the distorted shapes of the night. Inhaling the heavy perfume of city life—decay, pollution, leaves, and morning dew—she leaned a shoulder against the storage locker and peered down the length of the deserted corridor to the street, ever watchful for movement. Nothing stirred.

Yet inside a torrent whirled, and Maury's words drowned out the music in her head. "If you let them do their job, you could settle down and have a normal life."

"Fuck that," she hissed and bit her lip. Despite the trust she placed in him as her manager and lawyer, Maury couldn't know what it meant to be "on the government radar." Why should she consent to some watch list? Someone always monitoring her movements. Never free.

In her whole life, Aya had done nothing wrong, yet she'd been hounded every step of the way because of something a grandfather she never knew did and a mother and grandmother who capitalized, for their own monetary gains, on the continued American infatuation. A new revelation here—what the shooter really thought when he pulled the trigger; diaries—how the termination of a president would benefit Mother Russia; and photos—family and friends forever exposed due to association. Everything done to always keep the events from 1963 Texas alive. The sins of thy father bullshit. She didn't even know her own father, let alone her grandfather.

No, she'd decided a long time ago she'd live her life on her own terms. And that meant she was on the move again.

Aya paused before opening the trundled door of the storage unit. The scents of gas, dust, and mildew floated in the early morning fog that rolled in off the bay. Amazing to see the sky so clearly, yet visibility on the ground be so limited. She pinched her nose to squeeze off the sneeze. No use, it peeped out, and her eyes watered. She stole a glance over her shoulder, expecting the hairs on the nape of her neck to stand up on alert of danger waiting just around the corner.

Nothing.

Still attentive, she allowed her shoulders to slump a little. Relieved the tension. Relaxed, she brushed gloved fingers across her brow and through her hair, scratching the back of her neck. Then she stifled a yawn. So wide had she opened, the hinges of her jaw cracked in protest. "Oh," she said, surprised before bending down to peel open the garage door.

The grind and squeal of the rollers shattered the tranquility of the early morning. Aya stiffened in anticipation of lights flashing on and being found. Her ears perked, aware of the slightest noise. In the far distance, a car alarm. Closer, maybe a block or two away, a train rumbled down the tracks, followed by the angry bark of a dog. But nothing near.

Next to bare, the locker housed one item—a classic Indian motorcycle. Restored, the original colors of red and beige caught the dim light. Aya took a reverent moment to run her hand along the pristine finish before squatting to check the gas tank and fasten the saddlebags in place. Then her guitar, her prized possession. On a deep meditative breath, she double-checked the contents of her backpack: a couple changes of clothes, basic toiletries, and her laptop. Replacing the pack snugly onto her shoulders, she zipped her leather jacket to her chin, picked up her helmet, and placed it on her head before she wheeled the bike out of the shed.

Another quick glance inside the darkened interior confirmed she left nothing behind. There had been nothing else. She shook her head. The actions she'd taken today were impulsive, perhaps stupid. Time would tell. A courthouse. In broad daylight. Yet she couldn't regret her decision. She'd had to see Trip for herself. He fascinated the storyteller in her. Not just by the legend of Trip Vincent. There had to be something. She understood more than most things weren't always what they seemed or what the headlines revealed.

It had been a long time since Aya had been attached to anyone or anything besides her wheels or guitar to leave behind. Even longer since she actively pursued a meeting. Shrugging her shoulders, she continued down the lane, not bothering to shut the roller door. Such was life—a life she chose. On her terms. Her grandmother and mother, a pair of peas in a pod, might like to profit from the family shame and scandal, but not her. The murderous son of a bitch would rot in hell for the legacy he'd left the survivors.

Aya paused while her gaze swept left to right and back again. Leaving had become a routine of which she was a motivated participant. Occasionally, though, she would admit what used to be a thrill of a new start now housed itself as dread in the pit of her stomach. The fear of starting over and all she would have to do to survive—yet again.

Then the sad slant of the ocean gray-green eyes from a face etched in misery flashed in her mind. Such a vibrant man locked in a cell of Trip's own creation. Doomed for an action for which he had no control. Held responsible for others' decisions. She understood. Sorrow not yet mourned. Aya was moved and swiped at a spilled tear, which trickled across her cheek. Pulled by an invisible thread to this stranger who for some reason didn't seem so strange to her. Willing to risk a way of life she had come to rely upon, she would find him again. All in a matter of time.

Gripping the handlebars, she glanced at the wheels, ensuring they were good to go, and nodded. Though the bike dwarfed her petite five-foot-two frame, Aya wasn't daunted. She swung a leather-clad leg over the cushioned seat to straddle the large machine, her one constant through all of her journeys. She reached inside her jacket for her phone. The tips of her boots skimmed the pavement. She held the precarious balance. Removing her gloves, she slipped the tiny SIM card from the cell and cracked the mechanism in half, thereby severing the mobile connection. The pieces fell to the ground. Turning the switch, she kicked the motorbike into gear.

She cast her gaze from the bridge on her left to the warehouses on her right, mentally tossing a coin on which direction to escape the city. Drawn to his plight, she reflected on Trip Vincent and his fall from grace. To have ascended so high, only to plummet so low. Why his story in particular caught her attention, she hadn't yet taken the time to analyze, but he had, and she would. One of the many articles published about the superstar had regaled how his grandparents met on the golden coast of California. In the story, Trip had told of how his grandmother Elleah's voice sailed on the summer breeze, reeling in his grandfather, Reginald, like the fishermen in the bay. For that reason, Trip had made it a point to play a concert on the beach of the iconic Hotel Del Coronado.

But all that was before the tragic accident. Still, Aya bet, from what she knew of Trip Vincent, he would hold to that promise.

Aya nodded, loving the simplicity and romance of the Elleah and Reginald story. So, inspired, she'd written a song. Though not the first she'd written nor the first to sell, "Sea Breeze" was the first to reach a top twenty spot on the charts and launched her career as a songwriter.

The connection, the romance, drew her. The thread pulled her to a coast she'd never laid eyes on before. In that moment, the decision was made by the tilt of the front wheel. Lowering the visor of her helmet, Aya peeled off to the right, the vibration of the engine shooting along her thighs. She held tight with her knees braced and let the feel of the road release previous tensions.

Freedom to Aya came at a high price. Would she never stop having to pay?

But no flashing lights gave chase while she made for the highway. The wind whistled below the rim of the helmet, and finally, the long-awaited thrill claimed her. She loosened the throttle, the tires gripping the blacktop, and she lost herself to the moment.

****

Days on the road had zapped Aya's strength, never mind her enthusiasm. Her thighs ached, and her butt was tender to the touch. Non-descript, roadside cottages offered necessary respite. The salted sea breeze blew through the ends of Aya's pixie bob. Fresh air, aromatic with farm vegetables, rich soil, manure, and the ocean, surrounded her. She combed her fingers through the damp mass to massage her skull. The sleep, shower, and nourishment hit all the necessary elements. Now, on the veranda, breathing deeply of the moisture-laden air, she felt refreshed and refocused. Tomorrow, she'd go again.

Across the road, avocado fields stretched as far as she could see. To her left lay the open Pacific, leisurely hacking away at the California coastline, never offering up apologies for taking back to the sea what the ocean rightfully owned. So this was the famous California Highway. Yes, she could see why so many had written about it. Perhaps she would, too.

Aya smiled at her poetic prose and pulled a slender notepad from her inside breast pocket. She jotted the thoughts down, recording them for future reference. As a songwriter, every moment mattered. Every sensation, expression, emotion—pain, joy, passion—offered fodder for lyrics.

She slid the small journal back in its place, her fingers brushing the plastic edges of the phone. She held the cell in her palm and contemplated whether now was a good time to make contact.

"What does it matter?" she muttered into her drink, draining the contents and licking the pulp from her lips.

On the road, will notify when find new location.

The text message pinged, signal strength good from the new component. She glanced from the sunset to the first wink of a star and marveled at technology and people's absolute reliance on its every advancement. In her effort for freedom, she could certainly use a little less exposure to technology.

Despite the time difference, less than a minute passed before a reply from the only man she trusted, yet had never met, dinged back.

Running again? Why not wait? Where r u now?

She crossed the graveled path to the trashcan and smirked. Maury Wilkins knew she'd never tell him where she was, yet he always asked. What would it be like to meet Maury in person? Both parties would likely be disappointed. Somehow, cloaked in secrecy, they each lived up to the other's expectations. Remove the shroud, and what was left? A girl still trying to find her way in the world, and a man tied to the rat race, manager, promoter, producer.

She stared at the phone, many snarky responses filtering through her mind. Banking down her sarcasm, she tossed the juice container from two feet away and fist-pumped when the garbage met the mark.

Will text when arrive.

Maury had complied with her request to investigate the car wreck that killed Kurt Davidson. Even made sure Trip's lawyer received the vital missing pieces Aya couldn't believe didn't form part of the court documents. But he wouldn't understand the burning need to know—to see, to feel—seeking to understand in another what she felt in herself.

In doing so, by attending the trial, she had tipped her own hand and been caught on camera. A courthouse. Of course, she'd been recorded and recognized in all the media frenzy. Within a short period of time, whoever's job it was to scan those kinds of footage—likely no human involvement at all but some computer algorithm programmed for facial recognition—had found her. Again.

By the time she had exited the courthouse via the facility's backdoors and down the alleyway, a government vehicle had pulled up with two servicemen scouting the edges of the crowd surrounding Trip's limo. Being small offered some advantages. While they tried to blend in, she crouched low, turned her jacket inside out, and dashed through the crowd, caught a bus, and was out of the city in under an hour. Gathering her gear, she'd hit the road under the cloak of darkness, and only then achieve some measure of freedom.

Someday, perhaps, she'd likely give up the chase and fall to the government terms of her very existence—but not yet. She'd tried unsuccessfully a couple of times before. Unsatisfied, Aya wasn't ready to cooperate. To be held in any way responsible for something that had happened two generations prior seemed ludicrous. Acceptable or not, this was her reality.

No. She shook her head and rolled up her sleeves. Evasion was the best tactic. She had lost too many friends, jobs, and basic dignity at the hands of the feds to try it their way. What happened fifty years ago—the atrocities of her grandfather—had nothing to do with her. Yet this was a country that couldn't forget. Who could blame them? Still, the crimes of her forbearers continued to punish the descendants.

As she made to store the phone back in her pocket, it vibrated with another message. She smiled, turning her attention to the future instead of the past.

Travel safe.

Her songs paid the bills, and since she was his anonymous bread and butter, Maury needed her to be secure. That was the *only* reason she trusted him.

Chapter Three

The light from the parted shades sliced through Trip's closed lids like shards of glass. His hand, as though attached to another body, groped to find his face. Unconsciously, the pads of his fingers traced the scar. An itch like ants scampering fluttered across his skin. Bile rose in his throat. Trip hated the fact that another day dawned, and he lived to see it. He laid his palms flat against his sockets for an extra layer of protection against the day and to prevent further injury from the invasion of miserable sunshine.

He smacked his lips, trying to infuse saliva. "Shut the drapes..." he croaked, his voice dying with the effort of speaking to whomever had mounted the intrusion into the induced coma of sleep. He tilted his head away and flopped his tongue against the roof of his mouth, encouraging moisture.

A shadow crossed his lids.

"Trip, baby, come on."

The coaxing whine of the voice jiggled the rocks inside his head so they smashed against his skull.

"You promised at the club last night you'd take me out on the boat today."

The club—alone—but never alone.

Lifting his hands against the sun's assault, he shaded his eyes. Her silhouette tracked across the room. His brows scrunched against his palm. Unsurprised he couldn't remember her name, he racked his brain trying to remember leaving the club. Trip mentally shook his head, baffled by his lack of memory on where he'd obviously picked her up. Typically, he at least recalled leaving the establishment, and he always left with someone to take away the burden of being alone with his own thoughts. This could be the start of something positive. Perhaps, soon he would be able to forget everything.

Just like Kurt, a voice in his head muttered, and he flopped on his back. Angry. Kurt hadn't had Kurt as the reason. He did.

"I slipped home already to change," she continued with a small twitter of a giggle. "I have the most adorable boating outfit. You'll love it. I posted a selfie on Facebook to watch for me…"

Trip zoned out from the drone, overcome by an image of a younger Kurt fighting the sails on their yacht and tacking to the wind for speed. His best friend always smiling. His bushy hair flying in the wind gusts. Then, like the water lapping against the side of the hull, the image wavered between the pounding in his temples, gathering barnacles, just like their boat.

Fisting his hands, Trip screwed the cuffs of his palms tighter to his eyes to squeeze out the picture of gushing blood and a lifeless gaze. *Jesus, will it ever end?* The nightmare images. The constant reenactments in his own mind. He swallowed back the tears, coughing to clear the lump in his throat. That's what booze was for and exactly why he drank, so he didn't have to deal with those goddamned memories. Just how much liquor would it take to finally eradicate guilt's presence from his life?

The bed bounced, and whoever he'd picked up last night scuttled too close. The fragrance overpowered, like Hawaiian punch, the floral scent too sweet. Must have been a sale on coconuts. His stomach rolled, and his previously dry mouth flooded to activate a gag reflex. Trip swallowed to control the sensation, flexing his abdominals to hold back the heave. She brushed fingertips over a hidden scar, and he cringed. Resentment of his own creation prickled his skin, the intimate contact unwelcome. With an effort worthy of Hercules, he pushed up on his elbow and splayed his fingers apart to view the party gift from the night before. He scratched the fluff of hair on his chest.

Typical. He shrugged his shoulders. As he would expect. She looked like every other girl he'd brought home. Long-limbed, fresh, and tanned. Large, hungry eyes consumed her round face, the pert nose placed perfectly at its center. Through her animated expression, he could almost read her mind…but by the way she held her cell reverently in her palm, he guessed everything she thought was now posted online to share.

He'd developed a reputation in the posts these last months—cranky, sullen, withdrawn. Didn't seem to stop the groupies. They loved the tunes. They created a distraction. Everyone won.

He crooked a grin, acknowledging that she'd slayed the dragon last night. Hell, she'd even gotten back to his place. But she practically reeked of wanting more. Ambitious women like her who traded on their looks needed to hit the spotlight, and he'd proved easy prey these last months.

He knew he drank too much. Hated that he took advantage of his sister and her place. Despised the persona he'd created. Yet life seemed held at a distance for him now. Sure, Eva let him do his thing to a point, but even his sister had begun to question when he would find his feet again.

"When I damned well feel like it," he muttered. Trip pushed the blanket, rolling slightly away from the woman's touch.

"What, sweetie?" the tan dragon slayer crooned, leaning down, her breasts brushing against his chin. She laid a moist kiss on his forehead complete with a smack.

As though looking through the lens like a director for one of his music videos, Trip moaned. Time to get her out of the house before she found any creature comforts and thought she belonged. In his mind, he heard the chords unfurl the musical theme to match the moment. A pacing drum, slow movement leading to a crescendo.

He hoped Eva had already left for the day. Workaholic that she was, she seldom ran into him. Still, better to get the dragon slayer out without further ado, shatter her ambitions, and allow her to move on to the next mark. He drew a breath, ready for the words to accompany the melody.

Opening his eyes, he waggled his brows and winked. Then he made a point of giving Dragon Slayer the once-over. "No boating. Sorry, not today, love," he drawled, coercing the smile he used for the paparazzo. He spread his arm wide to take in the room and the ocean-front view. "Gotta work. Keep up the lifestyle and all."

Her pink lips pouted, and he wondered at the time of day. She was dressed for action, completely made up from head to toe. False eyelashes and heavy liner. Christ, did women really need all that? For a moment, he almost pitied her…then she spoke.

"Work? Are you kidding? You call singing in that mausoleum work? Everyone there belongs to the geriatric club." Her face pinched, lips thinned, and color flooded from her neck up. Even he could detect the rage boiling below her bronzed-to-perfection skin. "Get someone else to do it. You told me we'd go out sailing with all the gang."

Gang? Jesus, that's why he drank. He couldn't live up to the "gang's" expectation.

And as for the lounge…yes, he'd love to forget the gray gallery, but he'd made a promise a long time ago to host a concert on the beach where his grandparents first met to commemorate their anniversary in the fall. At the time, of course, the band had been intact—publicly, at least.

After the trial, in an attempt to restore and remake *Iron Clad's* reputation, starting with Trip, Arnold had landed him a summer gig at the Hotel Del Coronado as part of this "comeback" plan. Their music had developed a life on its own. In addition, Arnold had sent the other band members on summer hiatus. This suited Trip just fine.

The location, too, suited. The family owned a home right on the island where his sister resided, and he could at least feel physically, if not mentally, comfortable and accommodated.

Arnold had said the ties to his grandparents, who met when his grandmother was a lounge singer at the hotel, would work to Trip's favor and help create a new audience. All bullshit, of course, but who was Trip to argue?

"Nay, love," he said, stretching to allow the thin sheet to shimmy down his bony body. "Can't do it. I might be late, but I always show."

Her bottom lip jutted. She slapped a palm against the bed top. "But I posted already." She held up the bejeweled cell in the other hand for him to see.

Bingo. As expected, celebrity status. Something to name-drop later. He scrubbed his hands across the stubble of his cheeks and reached for the bottle on the bed stand. Never releasing his gaze from hers, he lifted the carafe and downed the remains of the spirit. The burn arose the rock star—the actor.

Patience at an end, he wanted her gone. He had to get this altercation over and done. Fast. This gal had a bit more temper than he was prepared to deal with today. In some small way, Dragon Slayer reminded him of his mother, Cherie—a woman to be absorbed in minute doses. Concentrating, he set the jug aside and flipped the spaghetti strap of the silken top off her shoulder. He licked his lips and pushed a hunger he didn't feel into his stare.

"Right on, doll. One more go before work." He cast his stare between her and his obviously rising member and back again. His chin jutted in the general direction.

She pushed back, mouth open, revulsion making her pale. "What? Are you kidding?"

His skin crawled. His reactions made him hate himself even more than usual. He craved to feel nothing at all.

"Where's the pout now?" His thumb outlined her nipple through the near-transparent sheath, and he tossed the sheet aside to show her the goods. "Come on, lovely. I've got what you want." He winked. "I'll give you loads to post about."

She hopped from the bed as though burned. "At the rate you're going, you'll be lucky if you don't have the clap."

He laughed. "Little late for that, I think." Ignoring the pounding in his temples, he sat up in bed. Mocking, he tilted his head and slapped a hand to his cheek. "What? Are you serious? I thought I used a condom." Scrutinizing the ceiling, he wailed. Then he bent forward to inspect his mildly engorged member for signs of decay. "Should I be tested? I assumed you were clean."

She gasped, and her pace faltered as she approached the patio door, grabbing her bag mid-stride. Hand gripping the knob and regaining some of her composure, she flicked her hair and called over her shoulder, "Fuck you, you prick."

The door slammed behind her, panes of glass vibrating.

"And another one bites the dust," Trip muttered and fell back against the pillows. Twisting in the bed with feet to the floor, he gained purchase with an effort to step—stagger—the few paces to the door and flicked the lock. Glad of the separate entrance to the beach house, which provided additional privacy, he drew the drapes and turned to find another flask he had stashed under the bed.

Bending, he tugged the pint out of hiding. Supposedly for emergencies. "Huh." He unscrewed the cap. Today's as good an emergency as any.

He didn't have to be at the lounge for hours yet.

****

Much later, the end of the flask meant Trip had to be at work. He stumbled over the back entrance into the lounge's kitchen. He reached a steadying hand toward the workbench to brace himself, flipped a carving knife placed too handy to the edge, and narrowly missed losing a finger in the process.

Straightening quickly and biting his lip, he shrugged. "Fuck. That was close," he said, more to himself, not seeing anyone handy. It took all of his concentration to remain still, though the room continued to tilt at odd angles. He chuckled and slapped a hand to his forehead, then lowered it to waggle his fingers in front of his face. "Would be lost without these."

A burp erupted from his mouth, loud and long. He laughed. Reaching down to position his hands in front of his belt buckle, he mimed an air guitar and moved his fingers to desired chords and strummed. Satisfied all was well, he resumed his progress, bumping a hip into the next counter.

"For Christ's sake!" the cook exploded.

Suddenly, a hulking form blocked his path. A man well over six-feet tall, blond with wide shoulders, stood with his feet spread apart, hands on his hips.

Trip teetered to a stop. His foggy gaze noted the blond giant blocking his path from ankle to neck before focusing on the face.

Some sort of Swede, he guessed. The line cook breathed through gritted teeth. He sighed and shook his great mane of white hair like an old work horse resigned to the task. He draped one of Trip's arms over his broad shoulders and heaved Trip to a chair in the manager's office a few feet away. "I don't get paid enough for this shit, man."

An accent made Trip aware the man was unlikely American born. Hateful at the world in general and angry at having to be helped, Trip spat, "You're lucky you illegals get paid t'all." Then he hiccupped, thumped down on the proffered chair, and pounded his fist on the heavy wood. "You—you don't like it here, you—you can swim the ocean home. It's—it's just over there." He pointed a thumb over his shoulder toward the beach adjoining the front of the hotel.

The cook turned in the doorway, face suffused in a glower, eyes bulging from a squared face. "I was born here, asshole! I'm as American as you."

"Sorry, man," Trip muttered under his breath, but the cook had already stomped off. Further shame mounted on his shoulders. Jekyll and Hyde. Had the Jekyll in him finally taken over completely?

His grandmother, Elleah, with her Trinidadian origins, would be mortified by his continued behavior. He could almost hear her voice in his head. "People who host love in themselves don't hurt other people," she'd say. "The more we hate ourselves, the more we want others to suffer." Trip hung his head, shamed. Why?

The buzz of alcohol began to recede. He swiveled his chair closer to the table, caught by the scrolling screensaver on the computer located in the middle of the vintage wooden desk. He knew the answer. Now, his grandfather's voice burned on his memories of his alcoholism and constant battle. Though Granddad was clean all their married life, he'd said never a day went by… "I think it begins with the hope that something, like a magic pill, can instantly fill up the emptiness—the less than—lack of confidence, affection…it's different for everyone. But what you want is relief, love, and fulfillment, and that doesn't come in a pill or a bottle. The 'fix' is temporary, and it's a trap."

"I know. I know," he said, chin to chest. He planted his elbows on the tabletop and cupped his face in his palms. "I know."

He must have dozed, because he woke with a start and a snort when his arm slipped off the desk. He yawned and stretched and leaned back in the chair, thirsty. In waiting for Arnold and what constituted his summer band at the hotel, Trip glanced toward the open door and contemplated going out to the kitchen for a drink. Water this time. But the thought of facing the personnel held him in his chair. Then a flash of yellow caught his eye, and he rolled the chair to the edge of the desk for a better look. The room sloped and swayed, reminding him he was not yet sober. Still, he planted his feet and cocked his head.

"I'm interested in the waitress job you posted in town." A husky voice drifted through the arched entry of the office. "Have you filled the position?"

Two people had paused just outside the office the hotel management allowed Trip to use. Reggie, the chef and lounge manager, filled the entrance. His beefy frame obliterated the flutter of yellow that had caught Trip's attention.

Trip flapped his hand. "Move," he whispered, though the big man couldn't hear him from this distance. He rolled the chair to the door and peered around the edge. His fingers curled around the door jamb.

Reggie cocked his head and reached to scratch under the chef's hat. "Ah, no," he answered. Then he darted a quick glance at Trip over his rounded shoulder.

Spotted, Trip rolled back inside the office to the desk.

"Not yet." Reggie heaved a sigh. "But now's not really a good time."

"I see." The throaty, feminine reply lacked the regret the words implied.

Peeking, Trip caught sight of two slender calves rising from walking sandals.

"I can come back. When would be a good time?" she asked.

The head chef moved his ponderous form, effectively blocking Trip's view—on purpose, Trip was sure. Reggie's shoulders lifted to his ears, and he exhaled his words. "Can't say—"

Vying for a better view of the legs and to whom they belonged, Trip lost his balance on the wobbly chair and banged to the floor. "Fuck," he slurred, rolling onto his hands and knees.

Reggie turned, a startled expression rounding his normally slanted eyes.

Instantly, Trip hopped up from the orange-and-brown tile.

Reggie's fist met his hip, and an angry curl lifted his upper lip.

"Reg," Trip barked. His hands moved to smooth back the waves of his hair. Immediately conscious of the livid scar, he fluffed his locks back over the side of his face. "How's it goin'?"

Reggie's lips softened, and his cheeks lifted in a genuine smile. "Pretty good there, Trip." The chef gave him a skeptical look, brows raised, his liquid brown eyes crinkling at the edges. "You need a moment there, man?"

"I-I'm f-fine." Trip cursed the slur, coughed, and tried again. "It's all good. You need your office?"

Reggie stepped out into the corridor and swung his arm toward the chair still inside the office. Momentary disappointment made Trip regret the quick evacuation of his sanctuary. The dusky tones of voice and shapely legs had him peg the female stranger as tall, luscious, and blonde. His typical companion. Quite the contrary, this pixie-like apparition gave him a slight nod while her firm, confident step crossed into the room. A tilt of her head, a sharp glance in his direction, and she accepted the seat. Not his type at all. Tiny, dark hair, wide-set, penetrating stare, and a mouth that quirked when she focused on him. Haughty. Her nose, though centered prettily, held a distinctive arrogant tilt, a complement to the pointy chin. The steely gray eyes dove into his without invitation, seeming to know him and not be fooled one bit by his tarnished veneer.

Trip rubbed his jaw, then scratched behind his ear, careful to keep his hair obscuring his facial scar. Had he seen her before? Perhaps at the club in town. The gaslight? She struck him as familiar. Where would he know her? Ice prickled his spine, and the dose of spirits he'd saturated himself with earlier seemed to disappear, leaving him sober and lacking to her inspection.

The silence became pronounced. It pounded in his ears. He couldn't stand quiet anymore. Stillness brought memories and... He wavered and laid his palms flat on his knees, fighting a wave of nausea and dizziness.

Her scrutiny meant nothing, he reminded himself.

She couldn't possibly know him. Though she seemed to see him when no one else bothered to look. Didn't he remember someone as striking as her with those wide, round, silvery eyes? *No*, he admonished, *she is no one.* Surely. Certainly, no one he needed to know. Perhaps.

Reggie gave him a nod, and Trip took the hint to leave the office. Then Reggie closed the door. Trip spun. The sterile white walls of the kitchen made the colorful array of food pop on the counter. Combined aromas of garlic, oregano, spices, beef, chicken, and fish made sickening bile rise up his gullet at a molasses pace.

She didn't know him. How could she? Yet—

"Hey, you okay?" The cook he'd insulted earlier approached.

Trip held up a palm in a gesture of peace, then opened and closed his mouth, willing words to form. "What's her—"

The cook had gathered his hair in a net and dressed, ready for work. He grabbed Trip's bicep. Hard. "You need a bathroom? Don't you dare hurl all over my clean kitchen. I don't care who you are."

Chapter Four

Aya swiped crumbs off the edge of the aged table into her cupped hand, then dumped the contents into a dirty bowl. In a moment, she'd take the dishes to the kitchen for clean-up. The comforting aroma of garlic and oregano emanated from the leftover food. In the end, she'd had no problem getting the waitressing job.

While she completed her tasks, Aya's mind drifted to Trip. Little to no planning precipitated her coming to the island. The lack of forethought did her no good. Though she travelled, like the gypsy her namesake implied, she did so with purpose. Except with this move.

Standing to the side, shielded from view behind the bar, she paused, shoulder against the door frame, looking out to the stage at the front of the lounge. She hadn't expected this version of Trip. The hurt, wounded animal. Raw pain eclipsed by rage. Her body slouched, and she lowered her head. Of course, she didn't know what to expect for she didn't *know* the man, only the music, and had assumed the rest. What a mistake this had been. Her hand covered her face. Heat flamed her cheeks.

Aya lowered her hand and raised her head. Coming here might have been a mistake but was easily correctable. As quickly as she had arrived, she could leave. She owed nothing to nobody, and by this time tomorrow, she'd be on the road again.

Defined by decision, she straightened away from the wall. Hers had always been a solitary existence. Why should she care about some fallen rock star? Trip had more than enough money, never mind an entourage to look out for him, like the large mustachioed Arnold, his business manager. The man's approach between the tables reminded her she had guests seated and waiting to be served.

Arnold came to stand at the bar, and his large, bulging eyes rolled in her direction. A ripple of wrinkles washed across his brow. His lips were lost in the volley of hair under his nose while his teeth threaded like a zipper above his chin. He resembled a man of ages long gone. The roaring twenties with jazz clubs, pin-striped suits, and speakeasies.

He twisted, and his gaze travelled from Aya over his shoulder to the front of the room, vacant except for the piano, then back to her in a heartbeat. "Quite the bonus for working here," he said, lifting a thumb to indicate the show to follow, and winked. "Not every day a rock star comes to visit."

Trip chose that moment to stagger through the door behind her, landing heavily against her back. In a whoosh, the air knocked from her lungs, and she stumbled forward, dropping her tray to allow both hands to brace against the mahogany bar for balance. Gathering her wits, Aya bit back a retort and bent to retrieve her tray.

Mark, the bartender, strode around the bar and reached an arm to steady her. "You okay?" He rolled his eyes at Trip, who seemingly oblivious to either of them, burped and continued across the dining room.

Color flooded the visible parts of Arnold's face.

Anonymity continued to prove itself a useful weapon. As a prominent figure in the music world, Arnold offered a persistent influence while the name Aya Rose meant nothing. Yet as a songwriter under the pseudonym Wilkes Booth, she—or referenced as "he"—was a reclusive, award-winning composer of some of the public's best-loved tunes. The irony of substituting one assassin's name in place of the one she was actually related to always provided her with an imaginary middle finger to the law enforcement officers who constantly tried to pin her down and place her under surveillance.

Though she seldom found things to laugh about, Aya almost giggled as she moved to the nearest table in her section. Maury confirmed today the closing of the sale of her latest songbook to Arnold. Nice to put a face to the name. But... She glanced at the faces at the table, taking their orders yet paying little attention, her mind elsewhere. Would Trip sing the songs she had written for him? Anxiety burned in her gut.

Her fingers trembled as she uncorked the wine and poured for the couple. The clatter of the bottle against the metal side of the canister when she laid it back in the bed of ice caused her to drop the bottle skirt. Trip had taken to the stage, and her heart fluttered with worry for him.

Low murmurs accompanied by a sporadic eruption of claps announced his arrival. He looked slightly disoriented and bewildered by the setting. Aya's cheeks flushed in embarrassment for him. The vibrant man she had come to admire from afar seemed removed from this shell who, as though blind, searched to find the piano bench. Shaggy hair fell across his cheek to hide the scarred side of his face, leaving the previous warrior-like showman vulnerable. The harsh stage lighting did little to soften the strain of the last year visible on his features.

His hands lifted to stroke the keys. Random tinkles filled the hushed room. Then he stopped. She caught her breath in anticipation. He rubbed his knuckles and looked out at the crowd, then back to the music on the stand. Rustling the sheets, he leaned forward, shook his head, and tossed a few to the side. Peering again, he nodded, and then...a symphony of one.

The people, the sounds, and the smells from the kitchen all disappeared. Only Trip and the piano remained. The songs blended, merging with a few note adjustments. Magically, he seemed to transform one of *Iron Clad's* classic head-banging pieces to an ambient blues number, and the previously uninspired audience fell under his spell.

Including Aya.

On and on, the opus continued for about twenty minutes but hadn't touched any of the newly purchased music, nor had he sung any of the songs she had written previously for *Iron Clad* at large.

Her stomach unclenched, and disappointment spurred her onto her duties in waiting the tables.

The music became background as he mostly focused on the band's early beginnings. *Safe*, Aya thought. No recent memories to muddle the content. Ending by slamming the cover on the piano, he stood, acknowledged the applause, and left the stage, making a beeline for the bar.

She glanced to the end of the room where Mark

had a tall glass waiting.

Not long after, the guests trickled out, and the restaurant fell empty. Even the patrons from the lounge retired early, signifying a work night. Aya finished her cleaning. Gathering her personal items, she moved to the edge of the kitchen and clocked out from her shift.

She hesitated in passing the bar when Mark offered her a drink. "I shouldn't really," she said, glancing toward Trip at the end of the narrow mahogany expanse. Warmth radiated at his close proximity, and she tamped down the unaccustomed attraction. Still, a quiver ran along her spine. She might be leaving tomorrow, but…no, she *had* to leave. He offered too dangerous a temptation. The kind of enticement she had never felt before.

Trip met her gaze and stared openly, appraising her from head to toe. "Go on," he said and nodded, as though she sought his permission.

Aya rolled her eyes, shook her head, and smiled at his audacity.

"Oh, don't mind him," Mark said, his brown eyes warm yet playful. "He'll either stumble off to one of the other bars on Ocean or go home."

Trip moved from the end of the bar to plunk himself down three stools away from her. "Think I'll stay awhile," he replied.

Aya leaned against the polished wood, her elbow balancing her weight. Other than the ping of pans and low murmurs from those cleaning in the kitchen, the place seemed empty.

Her forefinger grazed her lips. "Home?" She glanced at him, returning his frank stare. "You don't stay at the hotel?"

Trip shook his head. "They offered, but Sis owns a place just a few minutes from here." He gulped the clear contents in his glass. "My twin, actually. Though there's little resemblance."

"Too bad." Aya tilted her head, her finger tapping her bottom lip. "Pretty boy like you. More the shame, I'm sure."

Mark snorted and turned his back.

Trip raised his brows and swept a hand over his chin, scratching against the stubble. Then he nodded and grinned. "What's your poison?"

Aya pushed back from the bar and looked at Mark holding a glass and dishcloth. "Guys still ask that?" Setting her jacket on the next seat, Aya smiled and stepped up to sit on the raised stool.

Mark stood across from her and muttered, "He's got a limited vocabulary."

Aya laughed. Their interest warmed her consuming loneliness. "Aren't you off soon, too?"

Mark raised his brows. His gaze fastened on her, searching for another meaning. He quirked a roguish smile. "Sure. All the customers are gone. Reggie won't care if we have a drink."

She nodded. "Whiskey. Neat."

"Hard core." Trip tipped his own glass to drain the contents, drawing her attention once more.

Had she impressed him? Both of them? She didn't mean to.

Mark slid the stumpy glass across on a squared napkin. Then he leaned forward, elbow on the surface, chin resting in his palm. "You live far from here?"

She sipped her drink, focused on Mark but thinking of Trip. In his late twenties, Mark was tall, with swarthy dark looks, clean shaven, and neatly dressed. No doubt, she could do worse for a night. But then, glass in hand, she paused while her gaze travelled across to Trip. At that moment, he raised his light-colored eyes to hers, and they locked. The heat sparked in her pelvis had nothing to do with the warm burn of the amber liquor.

With decision, she tossed back the whiskey in one gulp and returned her gaze to Mark. She shook her head. He wouldn't satisfy the hunger, and Aya would rather starve than substitute.

"Sorry," she said and laid the glass on the napkin.

Mark smiled and shrugged. "Next time." He poured her another.

She accepted the drink. "Maybe." She emptied the contents, then lowered her voice. "But if you think getting me drunk will change my mind...you're wrong."

"I'm not that kind of guy."

Aya laughed. She covered her mouth with the tips of her fingers as the noise had erupted unexpectedly. She so rarely laughed the bubbling feeling felt strange.

"I am, though," Trip volunteered.

"No doubt," she replied and twisted to face him. She tilted her head to the side and shrugged. Neither would know she had a head for booze. Though she wasn't a drinker as a general rule. She lived a life where her wits were important, but she had found over the years she could hold her own. At the moment, emotions in conflict and having arrived on the island misguided on a whim, she could use a little forgetful juice to soothe the internal humiliation of shamelessly following a celebrity like some teenaged groupie.

Trip leaned closer, his sharp nose leading the rest of his body. His eyes squinted, and the line of his brow deepened. "Why do I know you?"

The hair on her neck rose. Feigning calm, she looked at Mark. "Two in one night. Does that line ever work?" Obviously, Trip didn't remember her from either the courthouse or from when Reggie hired her.

Mark stood and glanced from one to the other, clearly miffed. "For him?" He shrugged. "Or for you?"

His words bit, but Aya ignored him and accepted the refill. Mark gave the impression this wasn't the first time Trip had moved in on his perceived conquest. Too bad for both of them. She had no interest in getting involved in a pissing match.

She pushed the glass back across the mahogany. "That's good for me."

Mark slipped the cloth through his fist. "If you give me a sec, I'll walk you home."

She shook her head, hopped off the stool, and grabbed her jacket. "Thanks. No."

Trip grabbed her arm as she shrugged into the light garment. "You didn't answer my question."

Her heart skipped, and heat flamed. With an effort, she smoothed her face into the perfected look of impassiveness and tried to shake his grip. "Sorry?"

"How do I know you?"

"How should I know?" she replied and tried again to break his hold on her arm. He proved stronger than his scrawny frame belied.

"You don't know me," Trip said. His gaze raked her from head to toe. "You're not even my type with your impish nose and slanted eyes…" He breathed in deeply, snorted, and dropped her arm.

45

Her limbs felt too heavy to move. His tone and physicality left her feeling naked and vulnerable. Aya glanced between Trip and Mark. This wasn't how she anticipated meeting Trip "officially." Her organized life of flight, like a bird seeking destinations, always on the move between one place and another, seemed to crumble in this one interaction. Her pulse raced. She hadn't considered acceptance or rejection and didn't know where this fell.

She gulped and with supreme effort spoke. "We've established that," she said after a pregnant pause.

Trip tossed back the contents of his glass, coughed, and wiped a hand over his lips, dragging his fingers over his chin. "Then stop looking at me like you know me. Like you have the right to judge—"

"Hey, man, that's enough," Mark interjected, reaching across to take Trip's glass. "Leave her be."

Trip dropped his arm, his palm slapping flat on the surface. "She doesn't know me."

Everything stopped. Acting on impulse, Aya twisted toward Trip, hand cupped under his chin, and forced him to meet her gaze. "But I do know you," she announced and heard Mark's indrawn breath. "I know you're better than...than—" She stood back a pace to allow her gaze to travel the length of him, from his lanky, greasy locks to his disheveled clothing. "This."

"I'm sorry," Trip said, head hanging. "So sorry."

Her fingers fluttered in illustration from his head to his toes. "Consider where you come from. Musical legends. A proud family, yet you allow yourself—and your talent—to waste away...in what? A bottle? My God, you can't even handle your drink." She shook her head, lips pursed. "Shameful."

Not allowing herself a second glance and with pulse pounding in her ears, Aya turned on her heel and marched from the room, out into the cool of the night. She didn't slow her pace until she reached the café. Pausing at the foot of the stairs leading to her lodging, she gasped to catch her breath. Only then did she realize the free-flowing tears. This was why she was here. Drawn to him like a moth to the flame.

She swiped the tears. "No." The sound a gasp. She couldn't leave. Not yet.

Chapter Five

Aya didn't suffer fools and refused to feel the chump. So with a determined step, she arrived for her shift and shared pleasant conversation with Mark as though nothing out of the ordinary had transpired the previous evening.

During the day, as was typical, she converted her conflicting emotions into song lyrics and enjoyed the release. A brisk run followed by a short meditation left her renewed. Something had guided her. Something motivated her like never before, and she had to accept that. Coming to the island may have been misguided and impetuous, yet she was inspired by circumstances and surroundings, and in that she was building a healthy new songbook.

The glitz and dazzle of the Hotel del Coronado inspired old-world charm, and she applied different methods to her harmony. At the end of the day, how this translated across the airwaves depended on the artist who would ultimately purchase her music, but at this stage, she felt satisfied with the effect.

The soothing charm of the dining area clashed with the bustle of the kitchen and added to her anticipation of seeing Trip that evening. His woebegone gaze had haunted her dreams, leaving her breathless and aching. It was one thing to brush off the previous night's event to Mark, quite another if Trip chose to confront her again. If he put two and two together, he'd peg her as a stalker—and he'd be right.

She stacked the cups in the dishwasher cubby and noted the slight tremor in her fingers. Where were the effects of her meditation now? The ceramic rattled, the noise lost in the hubbub of crashing utensils, banging pots, the whoosh of burners, and rattle of pans. Fact was, she burned in expectation of Trip Vincent's performance. Aya concentrated on her breathing to calm her racing heart. *In, count to three. Out, count to five. In and out—repeat.*

She couldn't explain the draw to a man she didn't know. Unnatural, never mind unconventional, though she had never played by the rules.

Her mother had always said she had too much rebellion for her own good. Likely because Aya refused to participate in the anniversary gilding of the family humiliation. The slimy capitalization of familial tragedy. Shame flamed Aya's cheeks in memory. Even now, she could go to any bookstore and find their story in any number of volumes. How her grandmother profited from the retelling of her grandfather's role in murder. The sniper from Texas. How he famously took the life of the modern-day King Arthur and subsequently caused the country's fall from Camelot.

Aya wanted a normal life, craved it, yet... Perhaps regular and ordinary didn't form part of her DNA. Still, every day she spent outside the watchful, prying ocular of government officials meant she remained free. She had long since abandoned what lingered of her dysfunctional family members and struck out on *her own* path—on *her own* terms. She didn't have to accept the heritage left to her. She could create *her own* personal legacy.

The crash of cutlery against the stone floor brought her back. She caught the eye of Juan, the short, square-shouldered cook, and smiled.

He tilted his head toward his shoulder, brows raised. She had dallied too long. Customers waited.

Aya smoothed the apron over her pencil skirt, adjusted her blouse, and raised her chin. Just another day. She reached for the tray of water carafes and returned to the dining room. The strum of a guitar stirred tingles along the tips of her fingers. Just this morning, she had sent Maury music and lyrics to eight songs. He might not be able to sell them all, but one or two would rack up a nice commission. Choice was the key.

"A bit of a departure from what you've given me in the past," he'd said when she called to ensure he received the encrypted files. "More folksy. An age gone by."

"The return of golden lyrics." Standing at the window in her rented room, gazing out at the tourists, she grinned, enjoying the back and forth. The sea breeze carried the scent of salt and suntan lotion. Fishing boats bobbed in the distance, while the ocean lapping the wide beach made her contemplate Trip and how he transformed his music to suit his present circumstances. "I'm inspired."

Maury chuckled. "Well...if Wilkes Booth is inspired, I imagine I can be, too."

"There you go," Aya said, stepping away from the view to run a light touch over her beloved guitar. Her fingers caught the end of the wire and plucked a note. The single note filled the small space.

"Will you ever pick up any of these Grammys I've been collecting on your behalf?"

The awards themselves meant little, other than the recognition of her body of work. In an industry plagued by eccentric behavior, no one ever seemed to question why they had never met nor seen a picture of the elusive Wilkes, and that suited her just fine. She lowered the phone from her ear and checked the time, ready to close the conversation.

"They're more yours than mine, anyway," she'd said. "Enjoy."

Humming along with the guitarists, Aya returned to the present to focus her attention on the tables in her section of the dining room. Noting the bills tucked under the plate of a recently vacated table, she stashed the bills in her pocket while she cleaned, then on her way to the kitchen, pulled them out and placed them in the tip jar at the edge of the bar. She'd been fortunate in selling her compositions and didn't need the money. This always struck her as an irony, considering she grew up in a household which prized the almighty dollar above all else. Her face flushed recalling how often her grandmother would call a local tabloid to "sell" some deep-seated family secret in exchange for cash.

Tonight, Trip's band mates would join him. She walked in front of the raised dais where the musicians had assembled, awaiting their lead singer. The performer, an object of her own obsession, did threaten exposure, but she shrugged her shoulders, seeming unable to help herself.

Trip's story had fascinated her, because no one seemed willing to delve beneath the rhetoric to get to the heart of what happened that night in the hills outside of San Francisco, which led to the death of his partner and best friend, Kurt Davidson.

When Maury told her Trip's agent, Arnold, had purchased the rights to the song she wrote directly after the trial's verdict, Aya had to hear the lyrics sung from the man himself. Had that been the start? At this point, she couldn't say. She hoped he played the song tonight. Would he change the composition? She'd specifically developed the arrangement to match his clear baritone, even though most of his previous work tended toward grunge metal. Aya hoped he, as a solo performer, would branch out to meet his potential as an artist.

Despite his apology, the crass behavior didn't shock her. She'd been exposed to much worse. Within the slurred, inebriated speech, his voice held promise. Her song had been written to take advantage of the distinctive lift of the vowels in each of the words. The part of his dialect that marked him as surely as a fingerprint. He rocked her to the core. From the first moment when she'd stood across the great hallway of the courthouse. The subtle thrill that had coursed down her spine rendered her knees weak when he returned her gaze. His gentleness in the heart of the chaos. The wounded defenselessness he now tried to cover with coarse lurid rudeness.

Sure, she was a fan of *Iron Clad's* work. Despite the bad publicity, who wasn't? Given the decades of exposure to the media fascination with her family, Aya had always held herself above such frivolous emotions. With her anarchic life, she simply didn't have the time or energy to spare. Searching for simplicity had always been her goal. Yet she questioned the remote possibility of ever finding peace. Finding somewhere quiet where she could concentrate on her melodies would be her heaven. Some place like this island of Coronado.

No. She knew better than to become too attached to one place. Even here on this idyllic locale, she'd be found sooner or later, and then she'd be forced to live under constant scrutiny. She was here simply to alleviate her growing curiosity with this man, then she'd be on her way—again.

The crowd's reaction differed distinctly from the night before. The guitarist stopped and turned. Trip entered from the rear of the platform. His appearance resulted in a general intake of breath. Then a whoop from the back of the room caused a quick pause before the crowd broke out in applause.

Though his hair seemed slightly damp, he was dressed neatly in black and clean shaven. He smiled and held up a palm in greeting to their assembled reaction. He stumbled only once before gaining center stage.

Aya lifted a hand to cover her mouth to hide her grin. She surmised he'd either tried to sober up and not quite made it, or he'd taken a steadying hit before heading out for the concert. Empty tray in hand, she held it against her middle to quell the nervous flutters. Moving to the back of the room to stand to the side of the bar, she scanned her tables to ensure the patrons weren't looking for anything—food or drink. Satisfied everyone seemed sated and ready to listen to the concert, she leaned against the wall. She bent her knee and raised her foot to brace her weight and rested her shoulders, relaxed in stance, but tensed in truth.

Trip shook his head and seemed to examine the room at large. The black shirt smoothed the bony shoulders. The white T-shirt enhanced the pale complexion. The jeans bagged across his hips held in place with a wide belt featuring a too-large buckle. Looking freshly washed, the hair fell across his brow.

At first, he appeared confident, standing to the front of the stage. He opened and closed his mouth, then licked his lips. He lifted his hand, only to drop it back to his side. He squinted, gazed across the sea of faces, and seemed to consider something. Then, with a shrug of his shoulders, he changed his mind. Turning, he strode to the piano and took a seat.

A hank of hair fell over his left eye, and the confident, casual ease with which he brushed it back made her stomach tighten. Likely her reaction was a result of the length of time since her last intimate encounter and nothing more. She straightened from the wall. Now was his moment.

Her gaze feasted on a face made for flashbulbs. Even the scowling brow didn't deter from the vulnerability. Trip was the type of guy a girl would sneak out at night and cross to the other side of the tracks for—he simply created a challenge, probably why so many women had tried, yet failed, to hold his attention for long.

Mark, the barman, came to stand beside her. "You know your way around," he said, his chin jutting to the customers while he pulled a towel through his fingers. "Where'd you learn?"

"Here and there," she answered with a shrug. No stranger to easy banter, she managed to evade specifics while maintaining a friendly demeanor. There was no need to alienate Mark.

Reflecting on her brief encounters with Trip was

like toffee between her teeth. Her tongue wanted to happily work away at the sugar to enjoy the slow melt down her throat—pure, easy pleasure. In that moment, Aya's gaze locked on Trip, and she imagined him between her teeth. *Yum.*

****

Trip stared at his hands, noting the tremble. He could hear the breathing of the mass of people. The stench of consumed spirits and food caused his stomach to heave. Must he do this? Did he have to be here? Again. Night after night. Would performing ever be easy again?

The quick answer was yes. And then the long answer remained yes.

Yet he felt stuck. That waitress had gotten his goat the night before. He'd happily continue in his merry stupor, but she'd made him feel the disgrace of his family. Trip peered at the assembled patrons. Had he made the right choice on the first song?

Shaking his head to clear the momentary distraction of the slant-eyed waitress—definitely not his type—Trip drew another useless gulp of air into his lungs. If the new girl could sail past him like she owned the place, talk to him like she knew him, surely he, Trip Vincent, rock superstar, could at least pretend.

If only the fumes of patron-consumed liquor could slake his thirst—his need for another drink. He could easily order one—or two—to be brought to the stage. A little something to calm the nerves, perhaps? Mark would hook him up. No, better not. At least he was still able to walk. Any more and he'd likely make a fool of himself—again. Nothing new there, but Arnold had warned him only yesterday he'd better straighten up.

55

People had complained, and business would be threatened unless he got his act together and got focused.

"And that would have surely broken Kurt's heart," Arnold had said, his chin wobbling, rubbing salt in the wound.

"Like he'd even know," Trip had muttered and stepped out of the shadows to greet an elderly couple at a nearby table enjoying the flavors from a local vineyard before making his way to the stage only moments ago. Still, the wound burned.

He'd tried not to drink today. Tried and failed. He hadn't blitzed out, but…the buzz had settled to misty fog as Trip flipped music sheets, stalling. Expectant gazes bored into him from all angles, and there was no escape. A pitcher of water with lemon wedges floating on the surface sat on a table close by. *Blah.* He hadn't had a drink in a couple of hours, and right about now would be a great time for a double.

"What the hell," he said as his trembling fingers settled on a new song. He liked it. A piece Arnold had provided him only a week before. Seemed to be written just for him, but he didn't recognize the name of the author. He ran his fingers through his hair, careful to let the longer pieces fall over his eye.

The crowd seemed receptive. They'd listened and clapped to all the favorites. Perhaps now presented the opportunity to try something new. If it worked, Arnold would gloat, but… Trip smiled. It would be worth it.

Breathing deeply, Trip pressed his fingers to the keys, heart hammering like background drums. He'd only practiced the song a couple of times. Still, he admired the composition—the lyrics spoke to him—the simplicity so vastly different than the other works. The room darkened, the walls closed in, and oppressive heat swarmed. Sweat trickled down the side of his brow. He couldn't do this. Not a new piece. How dare he even try? Panic rising like bile, he squeezed his eyes shut to block the terror.

Sounds amplified, and restless shuffling from the waiting crowd surrounded him with a hum. Someone coughed while another snickered. Trip was the joke, the imposter, and the poser, and he had fooled no one sitting up here. Served him right.

He opened his eyes but couldn't focus. The swim of tears pooled, the room tilted, and his pulse rocketed on jet-fueled anxiety. He made to stand but seemed locked to the spot. Everything reminded him of his guilt. He was half—less than half—without Kurt, and not nearly enough. He feared he'd never be whole again.

"Oh, God."

Arnold would help. He scanned the room, unable to see. Where was his manager?

To the far end of the lounge where his gaze came to rest, motion caught his eye. That annoying waitress stepped from the wall next to the bar and captured his attention. Her pale features offered a striking contrast to her jet-black hair, dark shirt, and pants. Time stalled, and a quiet trickled along his nerve endings, bringing his breathing and heart back to regular. Though she wasn't his type, the sight of her calmed him in a familiar way. Why did he feel he knew her?

He focused and tried to absorb her tranquility. She smiled at him, then winked, quick yet packed with meaning. He sat straight and winked back. Her resolute stare fastened on his, held him, and he shook his head. Unwittingly, a smile spread across his face. He breathed in and out in time to the rise and fall of her chest as he imagined it.

"Okay," he whispered.

She nodded then, and as if on cue, he tinkled his fingers across the keys, getting the feel for the ivory. The delicate knocking of hammers against strings vibrated through the sturdy box, and the audience fell silent, expectant and waiting.

Her bow-tie lips lifted encouragingly. He relaxed on the bench, absorbed as though she had thrown a cloak of comfort over his taut body.

Then he shut his eyes, and for a moment, Kurt stood by his side, approving with a hand on his shoulder, nodding his head in appreciation of the melody. Not daring to open his eyes and shatter the illusion, Trip sang and played until he realized his fingers had stalled on the final notes.

Standing, he allowed the warmth of the audience's affection wash over him. A slight bend and a lifting of his chin acknowledged the crowd's applause and ended this session. The half hour had spun by. Forcing iron behind his knees to keep from falling, he strode from the stage to his dressing room and the waiting bottle he'd left there as a reward if he got through the night.

Chapter Six

Aya unclenched her hands. Her heart slowed to an almost stop, and her breath ceased. Her song. The one she'd written for him.

Just as a lover caresses their soulmate with a tender touch, Trip had sung her song in a masterful rendition. He'd made it his in the movement. The unique pitch of his voice in mid-stanza had brought a broad grin to Aya's face.

Returning to the moment, she lurched a step forward and banged against a chair when her heart slammed against her rib cage in a restart. Looking behind, she gasped to draw the breath back into her starving lungs. When Trip began, she had been standing by the wall next to the bar. She must have walked toward him as he sang. She had no memory of her forward motion.

"You okay?" Mark asked, coming to stand by her side.

Consumed in her emotional response, she nodded and turned to go into the kitchen. She tripped and caught the outbound door, narrowly missing crashing as another employee emerged. Having followed her, Mark grabbed her shoulders to pull her back.

He searched her face but said nothing before going back to the bar where a server stood tapping her foot.

A fellow worker peeked around the edge before

resuming her duties. "Watch yourself there."

"Oops, sorry," Aya muttered, rushing to a corner of the kitchen to make herself busy while she collected herself.

She brushed a palm across her brow, pushing the hair back. She hadn't expected to be so deeply moved. He hadn't just sung the words, the melody as she had proposed in the arrangement. But he'd sung as she truly intended when she wrote the piece, and yet he did it on his own. It was one thing to read the music and lyrics, quite another to breathe life into a number.

"I knew it," she said, stacking dishes.

"Knew what?"

Reggie stood between her and the sous chef line, dressed in his evening suit, preparing to greet the clientele. Thanking them for the patronage formed part of his evening routine.

"What?" She glanced up at his wide frame. "Oh, nothing."

"Well, I know you'll never move that stack from here to the counter by yourself." Tilting his whiskered chin, he indicated the near foot-high pile of plates she'd taken from the washer. "Get one of the bussers to take care of that. In fact, that's not your job at all. I'm sure you have customers waiting."

"You're right," she replied quickly, wiping her hands. "Sorry."

"No need for sorry." He wiped his hands on a dishtowel, then swiped spare crumbs from his suit sleeve. "I'm sure you saw the pile-up and wanted to help."

Aya preceded him back to the restaurant. By rote, she gathered payment, finalized bills, and soon, her shift ended. She bade her co-workers a good night, staring hard at the empty bar, then hesitated before leaving. Even Arnold had seemed to go home or at least left. Had Trip? She had no idea what his typical routine entailed.

Her stomach pinched. Casting a quick glance over her shoulder to assure she wasn't observed, with jacket clenched in her hand, she slipped behind the stage to the performers' dressing area. The dressing room reserved for Trip.

Pressing a palm to her middle, she paused a moment to draw breath. Then she brushed fingers through her hair, fluffing up the ends. Though she wouldn't consider herself pretty—God knew her grandmother had told her often enough she wouldn't be a girl to rely on her looks—she had a quality men responded to. Small but efficient, capable, and certainly determined, she seldom lacked for company. Her problem stemmed from retaining her hard-won freedom. After the first disastrous affairs, she'd learned a long time ago to leave before any attachment happened.

Just this once. Emotions high, still hearing his voice echo in her memory, she wouldn't deny herself. Not now. Not tonight. She wanted Trip, and since she was never one to back away, she moved her hand to the knob, turned the latch, heard the click, and pushed forward. The hinges barely whispered, and she closed the door with a soft snap. Heart racing, Aya locked the door behind her and briefly leaned against the jamb.

She licked her dry lips. Her actions hadn't gone unnoticed. His chin rose a fraction and his eyes widened. Yet he stood like a statue, watching, waiting.

A bottle, half-filled with clear liquid, paused on his lower lip, the spirits not yet reaching its mark.

Dropping her jacket to the floor at her feet, she crossed the small room in three strides. He met her gaze as though her arrival were expected. Gently, she gripped the neck of the bottle, sniffed the contents— vodka—then lowered it to the dressing table. She licked her thumb where a droplet of the spirits pearled.

"You can have that later," she said, reaching up to run the same thumb along the scruff of his jaw, ending on his full lower lip. "If it's still necessary."

At that, a smirk cracked the mask of his face. Then he dropped his hands to her waist. "What are you—?"

She cut his words short by pulling his head to hers and forming her lips to his. A small *ahh* eddied out the corner of his mouth before his palms rose to brace along her cheeks, his fingers threading into her hair to draw her to him.

She rose up on her toes and curled an arm over his shoulders to mold her slender body to his. Her breasts tingled as they pressed against his firm chest.

He eased back against the table, drawing her with him. Widening his stance, he snuggled her between his legs. This brought their navels level, and she pressed against him, dreading the annoyance of the layers of clothing separating them. The sharp flavor of spirits passed from his tongue to hers, adding to the burn and heat between them. Soap and musk mingled in an intoxicating blend. Hunger deepened the kiss, tightened the embrace, and fueled the fire to the point of being consumed. She ran her hands down his chest. In response to her touch, he groaned and slipped his fingers under the hem of her blouse. His tongue searched her mouth, seeking, exploring, and questioning.

She tightened her hold, threading her fingers through his hair, and matched his explorations with her own answers.

Then he stiffened. Drawing back, panting, he laid his forehead to hers, noses touching and eyes closed.

She ran her palm along the side of his face, behind his ear, and then brushed his unruly hair back from his brow.

Head moving side to side as though to a melody they shared, he leaned into her touch and opened his eyes. His eyes shimmered in the meager light. His hands dropped to span her midsection.

"You're smaller than I thought."

Taken unexpectantly by this, she chuckled. "Big personality." She ran her pinky lightly along the dark circles under his eyes, feeling sympathy for his obvious lack of sleep.

"Indeed." His lips quirked into a genuine smile, the corners of his eyes creased, and a splotch of color highlighted his previously gaunt cheeks.

Aya moved so their lips met. Then again in a lingering fashion to enjoy the fusion of their touch.

With the lightness of a feather, his expert fingers slipped under her shirt and released the back clasp of her bra. Trip pressed his palms against her ribcage and moved his hands around her torso until he cupped the slight weight of her breasts.

Her breath hitched, and she tilted her head back, enjoying his attention. She stretched her neck while his mouth blazed a trail of kisses across her jaw and down to her collar bone. Her fingers tightened on his shoulders while his thumbs massaged her nipples, drawing them erect like hardened pebbles. When was the last time a man had brought her such pleasure at the slightest touch? Need mounted. Her molten center erupted, and she ground her pelvis against his in a circular motion, matching his rhythm.

The clothing had to go. With a quick move, she grabbed the hemline of her shirt and drew it up over her head. The bra slithered to her feet.

She stood a moment, inches away, allowing him to gaze upon her. His scrutiny seared as much as his touch, and the fire blazed, ravaging in its heat. The flush spread across her skin and was reflected in his gaze.

He reached to unzip her trousers. With slow, deliberate movements, he eased the fabric over her hips, exposing the lacy top of her panties. His forefinger trembled slightly as it traced a line from her navel down to dip beneath the elastic until he reached the apex between her thighs.

A quiver wracked her core. She wanted this man like she had never wanted another. For him, she had risked exposure. But she would not give over to the sensations—not yet. If this first time with Trip was to be the last, she wanted it to be the best.

From her grasp on his shoulders, she massaged his biceps, moving over his chest to the front of his shirt, until she released the button of his pants. Pulling the hem of his shirt free, she lifted it over his head so it sat hooked behind his head and over his arms. Then she ran her fingers through the springy mat of hair on his chest. "Fair's fair." She smiled and dropped her hands down to his over-priced designer jeans, strategically ripped and faded to resemble aged denim.

He smirked and shook his head. "I'm a fan of fair play."

She was already aware he was no stranger to seduction.

"Fair trade, too." He stood to shrug out of the shirt hanging from his arms and dropped his pants as well.

"Commando," she said, stepping back a fraction and nodding. Undergarments were apparently an unnecessary hassle.

Trip laughed, a sound erupting from the deepest barrels of his chest, and his head fell back. He returned his gaze to hers, eyes lively and bright. "Impressed?"

Considering his question, head tilted to the side, Aya folded her arms in mock consideration. She raked her gaze from the top of his knees, along his thighs, to his protruding member, and up his chest to meet his gray-green stare.

She tucked her bottom lip under her teeth, then released it and ran her tongue along the edge. "Aside from the fact that you look like you could use a good meal…you'll do."

His brows rose, and his smile widened while his hands reached to encircle her waist. "You're not what I expected."

She tossed her head. "I didn't know you were expecting me." She unfolded her arms, braced her palms along the sides of his head, and ran her thumbs across his winged brows before brushing her lips along his.

"Expecting?" he mumbled against her mouth. "No." He drew away a fraction. The black holes of his pupils ate what was left of his irises. A flutter danced at the bottom corner of his left eye. "Waiting…I think…hoping, maybe."

The vulnerability made her gasp. The amount of air she breathed proved unable to sustain her thumping heart and the blazing need his words evoked. With the pad of a light forefinger, she traced from his cleft jaw, down his neck, over the contours of his chest, and along his chiseled abs, taking in every line of his rigid body.

When she returned her gaze to his, his eyes smoldered, and her body burned with an aching need. Red currents of fire lapped across her skin. His touch, everywhere he stroked—her waist, breasts, the crevice of her ass, down to the insides of her legs—all blistered with longing. Her insides melted, and she flowed with him. Then his lips returned to hers with a force she had never before experienced.

He pushed her panties down over her hips, and her legs lifted, wrapping around his middle. He reached his hand to cup her sex and massage the nub with his thumb. Her moan echoed his, flowing in and out of their joined mouths. Then he lowered his head so his tongue could lathe her nipples, pulling and suckling, consuming her, taking her into his being and making them one.

His own need pushed against her, and she reached to clench the length. The silky skin was smooth as she stroked from base to head and again, repeating, his panting gasps in time with her motion. She grasped his testicles and squeezed gently, tracing her thumb on the underside of the sensitive area until he released his grip and threw his head back and groaned. Then she led the member between her legs and allowed him to feel the slick of her wanting.

With renewed attention, he focused on her nipples, sucking to pull them taut. Then he nipped the end with his teeth and remounted the pressure. Laving and tugging, again and again, while his thumb assaulted the other. Each drag of her nipple tore at her core as though connected by an invisible wire, and each drew taut, a coiled spring ready to release. But he seemed to know this and eased his assault, returning to her lips, his breath gasping against her cheek.

He nibbled her ear, breath hot on her skin.

"Ahh." She basked in the torture of their nearness, frustrated they were not yet connected. It had been too long since her last sexual encounter, and never had she experienced this intensity.

His thumb eased into her mouth, and she suckled in rhythm to the massage of her grip along his penis.

"Oh, sweet Jesus," he uttered, removing said digit to slide within her moist folds.

Aya responded to his yearning desire and let her head drop, worshipping the multitude of sensations. Her need to be filled mounted like a volcano ready to explode.

He vibrated beneath her fingertips, his thighs tense. She wanted to spread wide and devour him whole to sedate her urgent need. She held back on the cusp of his entry and cupped his furred cheeks. Her thumb caressed his pillowy lips. She wanted to tell him she had no illusions, no demands. Nothing lasted. But staring into the great depths of his pupil-consumed, dark eyes, all she saw were yearning, regret, loneliness, and someone longing to be touched—not just sexually, but with his very soul. She understood.

Her mouth folded over his. The sensation shook

her inside and out.

She gasped when he entered her—warm, filling, and surprisingly gentle. Following his lead, they moved slowly, rocking in a rhythm of their own creation, caressing—a full enjoyment of the other. She already stood on the cliff, ready to fall. All she needed to do was jump.

Fingers splayed through the coarse mass of his hair, she bit her lip from calling out as the first shudder took her and lights like fireworks edged her vision.

His hands gripped her hips in a paralyzing hold while his body convulsed beneath her, sending further flames of delight along the inside of her thighs and up the length of her spine. She gripped with the inside of her legs and Kegel muscles.

She tossed her head, eyes closing, sensations rolling, crashing, and coursing along her skin, everywhere he touched, and longing in the places he didn't. At last, spent and holding him close in a straddle, a hand clasping his shoulders, she breathed. When she returned her gaze to his, he smiled. Small crinkles meshed the corners of his eyes, leading down to the contours of his cheeks, and his vulnerability touched her more than the bonding of their bodies.

A shaft of air delivered from the air conditioning vent above their heads sent a shiver over her exposed skin. She glanced up, becoming aware of her surroundings, and cold reality returned.

No matter how hard she gripped, moments ended, and she moved on. Nothing lasted.

In her world, it never could.

She touched his cheek with her own and followed with a light kiss. Then she scooted off his lap and dressed in a slow leisure heated by Trip's watchful gaze. Finished, she leaned forward, brushed her palm along the side of his face, pushed his hair back from his brow, exposing the scar, and kissed it. Then she touched his lips once more with her own in farewell. At the door, she paused. Hand on the knob, she glanced over her shoulder, soaking up his casual naked magnificence leaned against the dressing table, his fingers curled around the edge.

"You should get dressed." She grinned, the heat of his attentions still coursing through her veins. She turned the knob and stepped across the threshold. "Wouldn't want you to catch cold."

Chapter Seven

Talk radio rumbled softly in the background. For the first time in a long while, Trip listened to the business report and was interested. Not long ago, he'd paid attention. Years of being surrounded by the facts and figures associated with the long lineage of his banking family seemed to provide Trip with a natural understanding—through osmosis, he supposed. He grinned at the prospect of him ever holding a position in one of his grandfather's banks. The entrepreneurial spirit certainly helped with the financial aspect of running a band, but to ever pursue a career in business…no. His fingers twitched. They were made for strumming a guitar or playing a piano, not picking away on a computer. Apparently, he garnered more of his grandmother's artistic genes and happily left all the business know-how to his sister.

The station started in on the latest political blunder. "Not everything can be a scandal," he said aloud and reached over to switch the broadcast off.

Then he noticed the grinder on the counter. Roaming the kitchen, he found the beans in the freezer and proceeded to produce what he considered the best cup of joe he'd had in months. Resuming his seat at Eva's island nook, he enjoyed the rich flavor of the Columbian roast coffee. No cream, no sugar—straight up zing. Of course, the appreciation could also be chalked up to the fact that he was full-on sober. Another first in recent memory.

However, being seduced by a woman after a show wasn't a first, so why did he feel so different today—so normal? Complete in some strange way?

He lifted the mug to draw the liquid into the depths of his mouth, allowing the heat to burn on his tongue a moment to activate the taste buds before swallowing. Closing his eyes, he saw her scorching stare. The intensity of her gaze under the crease of her wide brow. The deliberation of her movements. She'd treated him like they'd been lovers for life, touching him with a knowing hand and consuming intensity. Not shy. Both generous and forthcoming in a way that evoked a response in him he hadn't experienced—ever. Nothing harsh. She aroused a profound tenderness, a requirement to protect and be gentle, despite a ravaging need.

He ran a finger over his lips and tapped his thumbnail against his bottom teeth. Elbow on the counter, he gazed through the window above the sink to the ocean beyond. The sea ebbed and flowed across the legendary golden beach, taking his thoughts, mixing them in the wash, and scattering them differently, reflecting his life through a prism.

He cupped his chin in his palm while his other hand traced the etching on the side of the mug. Did he know this woman? Where from he couldn't fathom, but the pull in his gut told him he was right.

Breaking him from his contemplations, Eva strolled into the room, hands in her hair, plaiting and twisting the long, blonde locks behind her crown. A thick, black, elastic tie hung from her lips. She approached, her nose lifted, sniffing the air.

Then a sharp intake of breath followed by a stumbled step showed her surprise. Her palms flattened against her heart. "Jesus," she gasped. "Where'd you come from?"

Trip laughed and stood to pour her a cup of the fresh coffee. "Upstairs." He set the cup on the counter. "You know, hanging from the rafters like all vampires trying to avoid the sunlight."

She stooped to retrieve the hair tie, which had fallen to the floor. "Oh, ha, ha," she said, standing, clasp in hand, hair flowing over her shoulders. "You didn't melt then."

"Nearly." He thought of the encounter. "I've been keeping to the shadows just to be safe."

He resumed his seat. Truth be told, he hadn't gone to bed. A smile curved his lips. He continued to find himself in a bit of daze from the night before, like a boy after his first time with a woman. Sudden insight to the greater understanding of what people spoke about so often came into clarity. How could that be? Sex was sex, wasn't it?

Eva left her hair to fall and slipped the elastic around her wrist. She placed a hand on her hip and leveled him with a stare. "You look different..."

Perceptive as ever.

He tried to straighten his face, but a happiness that had eluded him for such a long time filled the empty caverns of his soul. Instead, he continued to smile and enjoyed his sister's scrutiny.

She fanned her fingers at him and shook her head. "No, no, not different, better. Rested. Yes. That's it. You slept well for once." She smiled, and her eyes, the mirror of his own, softened, while her head listed a little to the side. "More like your old self."

"Like my old self," he echoed. To her credit, she never mentioned his drinking. Not once since he had come to live with her. Yet he felt the rub. His own judgment of himself. Aside from Kurt, Eva had always been the most important person in his life.

Kurt. Trip knew she wanted him to confide in her like they had when they were kids, finding themselves often their only friends as their mother flitted from one affair to another. But he wasn't ready to release the guilt, to discuss his friend and the final days—the fights—the anguish. Didn't know if he ever would be. And at the moment, the hinges on the box where he housed all his pent-up hurt and frustration over his former partner began to creak open. Maybe.

Even pondering the opening of that container of memories of his lost best friend made Trip crave a drink significantly stronger than coffee. The contentment began to flow away. A tickle at the back of his throat caused him to swallow convulsively. A meanness surged forth at the loss. "Not drunk, you mean."

Eva's face flushed, then lost its bright shine of moments before. She didn't deserve the harsh words.

Her face fell, and she eyed him a moment longer, gaze narrowed and brow wrinkled. Her lips firmed, and she turned to stride out of the kitchen.

It was true, though. Drinking had caused him to blank these last months, lost in the anesthesia of booze since Kurt's death. But when the sun rose this morning, Trip wanted to see it shine across the ocean. Wanted to participate in the break of a new day. Enjoy the undulations of pinks and oranges rippling across the dawning sky, turning it from indigo to purple to blue with casts of red.

Eva had left without her coffee. She loved him unconditionally, and he her. He stood from the nook, grabbed her mug, and made to follow her out. His sister asked for so little, yet she was always kind. He owed it to her to try to be kind as well—to himself and everyone else. He'd not only been neglectful but downright hateful to a lot of people who cared for him—Arnold, band mates. He wasn't the only one who had loved and lost Kurt. He wasn't the only one Kurt had targeted his final days, either.

In the living room, hands on hips, she had her back to him, gazing out the window. He brushed a hand against her shoulder and held the coffee in the other. "Can I interest you in some fresh brew?"

Her shoulders sagged, and she tilted her head to look at him. Taking the mug in hand, she lowered her nose to the steam. "Smells great."

"Course it does," he returned, giving in to the banter. "Best ever."

"Not better than mine," she countered.

The repartee so reminded Trip of times gone by when they were young. He could have wept with the relief of normalcy.

She turned, retraced her steps to the breakfast nook, took a seat, lifted the cup to her nose, and closed her eyes. "Umm." She sipped. "How're the shows?"

The dark-haired imp who'd seduced him crowded his thoughts of the night before, and his smile returned. "Good...so far." Would he see her again? "I'm sure Arnold will give me the full lowdown later this afternoon."

Setting the cup down, Eva stretched. A series of little pops accompanied her *ahh* of obvious relief. Color returned to her cheeks, and she smiled. Apparently satisfied, she took the elastic band from her wrist and proceeded to twist her hair into a bun at the base of her neck. "When can I come and see you?"

He shrugged, slouching somewhat in his chair to hang his arm over the rest. "Nothing you'd be interested in." His stomach cringed at the thought of his sister seeing him in the state he had been playing. But then last night and the new song, the old sense of belonging, being one with the audience. Shame flushed his face, and he strove for a nonchalant mask.

"I'm always interested," she said, standing. She patted the sides of her hair, then lowered her arms. The silence stretched while she seemed to analyze his face. "The only reason I haven't gone is you asked me not to."

Then she kissed his cheek gently and walked to the sink to rinse her mug. She glanced over her shoulder. "Mom's coming." He made to leave the kitchen. "Thanks for the coffee."

"Stacie?" He choked on spittle caught in his throat and lurched up from his chair. "Wait. What?"

She strode down the hallway. "You heard me."

He shook his head and followed his sister through the house where she collected her briefcase and jacket from the front foyer. "Stacie—Mom, here? Why? When?" He had sputtered so much he wiped the back of his hand across his mouth. "I thought Mom was with Gran and Gramps on the plantation."

"She's making her rounds." Eva paused with a hand on the doorknob. "You know how she is. Likely on the lookout for the future 'ex.' She knows you're here, so…two birds, one stone."

"No, really."

"Come on, Trip. She's our mother. She's worried about you." She laid her case at her feet while she shrugged into her light jacket. "It's your fault. You should have let her come to the trial, then she'd be done for a while."

"She can't," he said, feeling like a school boy again. All decorum and self-effacing, faux-indifference fleeing in light of having to face his starlet mother. He wracked his brain for an excuse. "We're a full house, anyway."

Her brows rose.

"With Cousin Wendee and me here in the house, there's no room." He placed a fist onto his hip. The reminder their cousin Wendee, who worked the front desk at the hotel, also occupied the house meant Stacie wouldn't have the run of things.

Her laughter tinkled in the morning sunshine streaming through the open door. She picked up her case. "Okay." She shook her head. "That's three of the six available rooms. Gran and Gramps bought this place specifically for large family gatherings. See how far that explanation gets you."

Eva opened the door and stepped down the stairs. "Mom's coming, get used to it." Pausing at the bottom, she turned to face him. "Cousin Wendee's all but living on the houseboat now with Toby. They'll be married before long. Frankly, I don't know what the holdup is on the date, but soon, I'm sure." She began striding down the lane to the car. "Gran doesn't want to go to New York straight away and is really looking forward to seeing you."

He grabbed the sides of his head, pulling at his hair. "Gran, too?" She was the one person in his life he couldn't lie to—couldn't fool.

"Gramps never lets her travel alone." A chuckle threaded through his sister's voice. "One big family reunion."

Heart hammering, Trip stood and fumed on the stoop a few minutes after his sister left. What was he thinking with this sobriety thing? Feeling exposed, now he definitely needed a drink.

Then, as he stood there glaring after his disappearing sister, like mist on the water, the image of a woman across the asphalt crowded his mind. She gathered shape and structure, then Trip saw the laser silver of her eyes, wide and staring. *He did know her.* The imp who'd seduced him after his show was the very same who had come to his trial. His moment of grace from the chaos.

Chapter Eight

Aya sat at the small window seat and strummed her guitar. Water splashed against the sill and rolled in dashed rivulets to pool along the pane before dropping to the ground. The patter offered comfort and cooled the previously stifling air. One knee raised to balance the guitar, she tapped the tips of her nails against the bridge of the instrument, the interplay in step to the rhythm of the rain.

The scarred device—a gift from her dad before he took off when she was six—had seen its fair share of adventure over the years, yet it held up. Worn with love, she mused. Shame her dad hadn't stuck around or ever tried to maintain contact, but the family drama proved too much for him. Reflectively, she tried not to miss him, though she'd barely known him.

In some ways, she must have taken after him with her itchy feet. Constantly on the move, evading any long-term connections. Even now, she was sure even if she wanted to, she'd likely not be able to locate him. Perhaps just like him, then. In fact, her name—which he chose, according to family lore—meant gypsy after all. What would anyone expect?

Tangled memories of fights, tears, laughter, stories, and abandon added to the overcast of the day. A thick fog of subdued emotion. Melancholy weighed upon her shoulders as she scribbled down a couple of sad lines of lyrics in her notebook. She never knew when something would take shape. Perhaps a ballet. She wanted to whip out a hard-core, head-flinging rock anthem, but that wasn't going to happen today. Content to let the weather provide percussion, Aya changed chords and strummed again.

Of all the places she'd been in the last years, the island of Coronado proved one of the most serene. Calm pervaded, even when a mass surplus of emotions swirled within her. Hard to belt out an emotional musical tirade when the place made a person so content. She breathed deeply of the moistened air and allowed her shoulders to relax.

Contentment didn't normally describe her life in general. Never had. Though she hadn't always been on the move. There had been a period of her life when she thought she could sidestep the historical comrade communist cloud that blanketed her family. Years ago, never political and basically still a child, she'd loved a man and assumed they'd build a life together. Brought up to it, she'd become well-accustomed to hovering authorities and scrutiny. She'd even learned not to travel too far, be involved too much, and as a reward, she'd been left alone to build her own life quietly. Or so she thought.

Then the fiftieth anniversary of the shot that stunned the globe came around, and her grandmother and mother decided to cash in. Not that any red-blooded American would ever let the story die. The untimely death of a president during office, a time marker in itself, the assassination of an idealistic president indicated the end of the new Camelot well-worth remembering. Though it had—for a time—seemed to

Aya that she could be forgiven for being the granddaughter of a modern-day Pontius Pilot. But then came the "tell-all" book, updated movies, documentaries, and even a television miniseries. Interviews and cash flow all marshaled and managed by her grandmother.

That she may never have the opportunity to ever see that woman again.

Aya had, from a young age, structured her life avoiding the limelight. A master at blending, always ensuring no one took notice. What happened two generations before didn't involve her. How could it? But when she and her fiancé were pulled from a concert and publicly humiliated, like her father, her boyfriend had had enough. So sorry, he'd said, eyes misty. He just couldn't do it.

Exactly like her dad, he'd walked, and she never saw him again.

"Good riddance," she said, fingers clamped on the neck of the guitar.

In retribution, Aya had sold the engagement ring, bought her motorcycle, packed only the items she truly loved or had a need for, and wrote a note to her mother. "If you have any love in your heart, don't look for me—ever." And she'd left, too.

She'd supposed, in the years that had since passed, she could again resume some form of normal life. Her breath caught as her stomach clenched in fright. A constant anxiety of having what she built be ripped from her again had kept her moving. She swiped a rogue tear while her gaze tracked a sea bird circling the ocean in search of food. She saw herself in that bird. So long as she was on the move, she'd be safe. Never truly depending on anyone or anything. Circling, but never settling for too long. For when the bird landed, it'd be at the mercy of everyone—the predators on the ground. But hovering above, the gull, like her, lived free.

"If my heart takes flight," she sang softly. "If I sing from my soul…will you fly with me, my love…walk away from all control?"

Aya hummed as she opened her laptop. She plugged in the receptacle from her guitar and launched the music composition program. Starting a new file, she quickly named it "Live Free" and leaned against the piled pillows. Closing her eyes, she strummed again. The program recorded the notes she played to the electronic grand staff paper.

She paused the humming to lick her lips and thought of Trip. Eyes closed, she ran a finger over her still-moist mouth. A sigh escaped. He certainly knew how to kiss. Like a woman starved, she ached for more. Though he hadn't been the first man she'd seduced, he certainly was the first intentional conquest. Stalking sounded like too strong a word. Concerned. Yes. But why? Inexplicably, she found herself drawn to him, first as a curiosity, then because of the music. But now—

"Oh, I don't know," she murmured, opening her eyes and lowering her knee to stamp her foot to the floor.

She sat up. The sea bird had disappeared from view. She scanned the small rented room. A two-cupboard kitchenette, small sink, and mini-fridge bordered the entrance to the bathroom, equally tiny. The remaining space offered enough room to fit the double bed and an armoire. But the window seat overlooking the vast ocean captivated Aya. Creative juices broke with the tide. Despite the location, rear side, above a café—which opened for business at six, meaning the bakers arrived at four thirty with their preparation including banging utensils—creativity seemed to radiate from every corner. Inspiration and the aroma of freshly ground coffee fueled every breath. For years, she hadn't touched the stuff, but the tantalizing scent got the better of her, and presently, she wondered how she ever lived caffeine free.

When the owner asked her on the stairs yesterday to let him know about next month, for the first time in a long while she'd hesitated. Here on this island, she could find a home. Her heart longed to spring roots like an anchor, holding her firm.

Yet it was time to move on. Trip had sung her song.

Aya rolled her shoulders and set her guitar to the side. Yes, she'd accomplished what she came for. To meet the man who fascinated her musically and personally. If she stayed, she'd be giving in to the scrutiny that came along with such a decision. She had no doubt "they" would find her sooner rather than later. Then what?

"The sins of thy fathers…"

The alarm from the cell phone chirped, and she stood. The evening shift started in an hour.

****

Trip gripped the to-go coffee cup like a life preserver. The small tremor in his fingers caused him to tighten his hold on the cup. He hadn't had a drop of booze since the encounter the night before and didn't want any. Well, "want" being a liquid term, threatening his resolve. As evening settled in, he had started to feel the lure. Obtaining a bottle would be easy, drinking it even simpler, yet he didn't want to black out. Just the opposite. What he wanted was to see this woman through sober eyes and confirm she was nothing of fascination. With a clear line of sight, he would see just another one-night stand—forgettable, like all the others.

Entering through the kitchen area of the restaurant/lounge, Trip threw the empty paper cup into the trash. It skidded across the lip and landed on the other side. So much for basketball. He smiled. He'd never been much for sports.

The audience apparently agreed. The giant blond line chef stopped his food prep, placed a hand on his hip, and stared. Trip knew the man was waiting to verify two things—one, if he was drunk, and two, if he would pick up his own trash.

Tossing the man a wink and a shrug, he bent to retrieve the paper cup and placed it dead center in the trash. "There we go," he added and smirked.

His co-worker snorted and turned back to the prep table without further acknowledgement.

Trip proceeded to the entrance to the dining room. Dinner guests had just started to arrive. He wouldn't go on stage for another hour. He scanned the area, searching for her. Just when he thought she might have the night off, her tight little body skimmed by on her way to the bar. She hadn't noticed him. Or at least he didn't think so, else she would stop, wouldn't she?

He couldn't recall her name. Not unusual, but an unaccustomed sense of unease settled in his gut. A feeling of self-consciousness he hadn't experienced since grade school. Even his palms were sweaty. If only he could pass a note to a friend, who would give it to one of her friends, and then someone down the chain would provide the answers. He lowered his chin to his chest. He wasn't a kid anymore, and his only friend was dead.

Trip leaned against the door jamb and pushed his sleeves up while his fingers tightened into fists. He sucked in air through his nose and forced back the rage. Pushing his shoulders back, he lifted his head and unclenched his hands.

The barman, Mark, chatted while he poured the drinks. She wore black well. Fitted dress pants, a T-shirt, and vest overlaid made her skin appear creamy, devoid of any blemishes. Bared arms were well-formed, not scrawny. Her dark, short-cropped hair had a jagged cut, the ends tucked behind flower-petal ears. Small studs glittered from the lobes. He closed his eyes, recalling her smell. Earthy and raw. A pheromone more intoxicating than liquor. Their encounter seemed to him akin to capturing a lightning bolt. Together they'd danced with the blue light until it exploded, leaving him in awe of the experience. But why?

He watched the exchange of small talk. She laughed at something Mark said. Trip curbed the urge to interfere. Jealousy curled his insides. He pushed a hand deep in his pocket. Why should he care? Really, weren't her eyes a little too far apart, her pert nose representative of someone snooty? His gaze skimmed lower. Compact and tight, legs shapely. But for sure, her breasts were at least a size too small for his liking. And yet here he was envious that he wasn't the one making her smile.

He pushed up from the wall to stand in her path when she approached the kitchen, tray full of empty plates.

She stumbled, then stopped. Color bloomed on the apples of her cheeks. Her gaze caught his as she backed through the double door and into the kitchen.

He forced nonchalance. "Hey," he said, stepping through the same door, and leaned a shoulder back against the wall.

She nodded but said nothing further. In the staff-filled, busy kitchen, she didn't flicker recognition.

He ran a hand through his hair. Really, she should be glad he remembered her. At a loss what to do next, he stared after her as she dropped the order off.

When she exited to the dining room, he remained, mouth open. "Wait, what?" he muttered under his breath. His palm brushed across the stubble of his chin, and he licked his lips.

Glancing around the assembly of chefs and line cooks who stared openly, Trip turned and left. Confused, he re-entered the dining room and peeked toward the bar. Despite the salivating urge, he resisted the pull of going over and ordering his favorite whiskey. Perhaps he ought to just go to his dressing room and get ready, but he didn't want to be alone. If he wanted to be sober for the performance, he had to avoid certain pitfalls. But why? He couldn't define what motivated him toward sobriety today, other than the mystery of this woman. Maybe Arnold would know her name. Yet he didn't want to involve his manager.

Nah, he could do this.

With an air of confidence, she sailed back across the room, this time seeming to move toward him. He smiled, elbow on the bar counter, a thumb hooked through his belt loop, and crossed one ankle over the other. He lifted his chin as she approached, but she seemed to take little notice. She coolly sidestepped him and proceeded into the kitchen.

A soft chuckle caught his attention, and he turned his head in time to see Reggie share a look with Mark and try to cover by coughing into his hand. While the bartender turned his back, the line cook shook his head and followed the girl into the kitchen.

"What the fuck is going on?" Trip straightened and dropped his hands to his sides.

Within moments, she backed out through the double swinging doors. Heaped plates of food arrayed on her tray, which she held aloft in one hand while the other gripped the portable tray table.

Discomposed, Trip grabbed her arm. "Hey."

She evaded, and the tray wobbled. Practiced, she righted and rebalanced, then glared at him. "What do you want?" she hissed. Her stare shot from him to the waiting customers and back. "I'm working."

"I want to talk to you," he replied, dropping his hold and stepping back from her scowl. This was not the reception he had expected. In his experience, women were delighted when he took an interest, especially the next day. What was her problem?

She glanced over her shoulder, first at Mark and then into the kitchen, then out to the dining room to the waiting guests. One brow rose, her grey eyes electric. "Why?"

"Because..." The word hung in the air.

What could he say? He wanted to reassure himself she was a nobody, and he could walk away. Now, with the moment at hand, that didn't seem correct. As her wide, round eyes continued to stare, he saw her again across the foyer of the courthouse where they'd formed an invisible connection. The depth of her gaze warmed him, despite her outward cool. Someone who understood what he continued to be baffled about. She held the secret, and he wanted to know.

Her foot tapped, then she started to step away. "I'm busy."

"No, wait," he said, a plea in his voice.

"This tray isn't getting any lighter."

He growled under his breath, lifted the tray from her, and refrained from commenting on the weight of the platter as he balanced it between his two hands. Grunting, he marched over to the waiting table. Performer's smile in place, he served the guests, making idle chitchat. Conscious of her watchful gaze, lips parted in a near grin, he turned, and taking her arm, escorted her to the hallway linking the lounge to the main body of the hotel.

In a darkened corner, he turned her to face him, hands resting on both of her forearms. "Why were you at the courthouse?"

Chapter Nine

Aya firmed her shoulders and clamped her lips together. There was nothing to say. Goose bumps rippled along her skin, and her core temperature dropped. Fear gripped her. She couldn't put to words what she didn't understand herself. She folded her arms across her chest and tapped her foot, waiting. This hid the tremble in her fingers and the quiver from her stomach, which robbed the moisture from her mouth. Staring straight ahead did nothing to foster calm. Trip's shirt hung loose across his too-thin shoulders and flopped open about four buttons, revealing the lightly furred chest she recalled far too well. Her palms tingled from the memory of their springy touch.

Yes, she definitely wanted him still but had not expected him to pursue her. She hadn't anticipated he'd remember, or that her seduction would even matter to a man well-known for his sexual appetite. Any kind of relationship, however brief, made her vulnerable to detection.

Relationship, huh.

Any conceivable explanation escaped her. His nearness brought a shortness of breath. She couldn't think. Besides, she'd already wrestled the "whys" for most of the day—why did she track him down, why was he the object of her obsession, why did she seduce him, and now that she had, why didn't she just go?

Leave. Create a sweet memory and move on. Having determined no logical justification, she'd simply given up and walked to work in the drizzle.

How had he even remembered her from the courthouse? Their gazes had locked for a mere moment.

She shook her head and bit the inside of her cheek. Any which way the motives rattled around in her head, it all came out wrong. Stalker? The word stung. Had the crazy that enveloped her family for generations sprung upon her now? How could she admit personal feelings to this playboy? The deep-in-her-marrow attraction. The understanding of souls. As much as she wanted him, like a candy craze, she couldn't give in. She couldn't express the words. Couldn't understand the thoughts or feelings.

Even now, in the throes of fear of exposure, his fresh scent of soap and dewy mist from being outside in the rain made her insides quake in longing. How easy it would be to entice him into a darkened room...yet...

"It *was* you." Trip lifted his finger to point. Close to the tip of her nose, the digit filled her vision. Then he hooked the end to curve under her chin, prompting her to meet his gaze. "Tell me," he coaxed in a gentle tone.

She couldn't. Jerking her body, she twisted out of his hold. "I have to go." Time's up. Like her father had always told her, "When you get what you want—get out. Don't wait around for it all to go sideways." Solid advice. And her dad would know. When he left, he'd never looked back. Now, Aya had gotten what she wanted—Trip had sung her song, and by the look of today's sobriety, was doing better, getting stronger every day.

She snorted and tossed her head. What a fool. He

didn't need her. Truthfully, she couldn't help him even if he did, considering she couldn't help herself. She'd been a momentary sucker to think he did, in any way, need her—he had people for all of that. Someone to fill every requirement.

"Don't." His palms cupped her cheeks. "Tell me. I must know." His darkened gaze held hers. "You can't know what it was like."

She could, indeed.

"Day after day. So much hatred. People I thought I could trust turned on me." He released her face to scrub his fingers across his eyes, then pinch the bridge of his nose. "The press and public had already played judge and jury. Nothing I said mattered, and goddamn it, nothing could bring Kurt back."

She stared, scrutinizing his face, and lifted fingers to stroke his cheek, then dropped her hand to her side. Drawing breath, heart hammering, she decided. "You lied," she blurted. The words jumped, harsh, merciless.

His eyes widened, and his mouth formed an O before flattening. He squinted, lines gathering at the edge of his lids as his gaze hardened to match his firmed lips. "What did you say?"

She should just walk away. Now. She'd said and done too much already. Aya told herself she didn't owe Trip anything. Still, she couldn't go. She did understand. He had to get honest with himself if he was going to come back from the depths. She licked her lips and folded her arms. "You heard me."

Whip fast, he grabbed her upper arm, his fingers like a vise on her sensitive skin. "What are you talking about? Who are you?"

The menace in his voice doused the lust from only

moments before. The threat propelled her. She yanked on her arm, but he wouldn't relinquish his grip. Heat flamed where the cold had been. Nose tilted toward the ceiling, she looked up at him, meeting his glare. "You lied—you weren't even driving that night. There were opiates at the scene of the crash. You may be a boozer, now at least, but you're not a user. No blood tests support that." Using her free hand, she grabbed his other arm and twisted it around, revealing smooth skin never marred from needles. "The same can't be said for Kurt. You took the rap out of guilt. You had a druggy partner who wouldn't go for help."

She gulped air, her chest heaving. "Now, you seem determined to go down the same path. Only you'll swim there loaded with booze."

He released his grip and staggered a step back. "Who do you think you are? How? Where'd you...?"

He reeled as though she had hit him, and she longed to take him in her arms and soothe. But that wasn't her way. Never was.

Aya hadn't managed to evade the authorities this long without making some key contacts, keeping one step ahead whenever she could. Her experiences had long since taught her to read between the lines. Weeks before the crash, shortly after they took one of her songs to gold on the charts, the news reported the nasty break-up of Kurt and his long-time girlfriend. Kurt's behavior seemed to spiral out of control. Reporters followed Kurt continuously and released news items on how Kurt had held *Iron Clad's* purse strings and been careless with the earnings. Rumors circulated, and concert dates had been cancelled. More speculation of Kurt entering rehab for drug addiction fanned the front pages of the gossip magazines.

Keen to sell *Iron Clad* more songs, Maury had tried to dissuade her based on Kurt's substance abuse. "Not only will he bastardize it, it'll stain your name as well," he'd said. But she had never written the song for Kurt. It had already—always—been for Trip, to bring him out of the shadows. A gift returned for a kindness shown to a young girl when she'd needed it most.

Aya lowered her head, remembering walking the streets of New York, guitar on her back, aimless, not knowing where to go or what to do when she'd first fled her home and the oppression of constant surveillance. It was while Aya was strumming on a street corner, box open and jamming for loose change that a woman had approached. For no known reason, the woman offered her lunch.

Starving, Aya agreed.

Where she had expected to go to a café, the woman took her to her penthouse apartment and in a cozy kitchen made her a delicious meal by her own hand. "Reggie won't be home for hours, and the grandkids, no longer kids really, are out..." She fanned long fingers in the air. "Well, somewhere." She smiled, a blush making her face even more ethereal.

Aya didn't dare to speak, fearful of being cast out.

"I'm Elleah," she said with an exotic accent. "You play beautifully."

"Thank you," Aya managed.

"My great love is music, and I can tell it is yours, too." Then Elleah had told Aya the story of how she had once run away. "To the loveliest place ever. The southern tip of California." How she had sung and eventually met her husband. "It's magical there. So much so we have a cottage right on the beach where we fell in love."

Aya stood transfixed. Then the noise of a crowd shattered the serenity of the moment. Teenagers, a boy and girl—close to her age, maybe slightly older—crashed into the kitchen, not even noticing Aya's presence. They launched in unison about their day, until the boy stopped, turned, and met Aya's stare.

"Who are you?" he said, eyes the color of the ocean current swirling with life.

She lowered her eyes. "No one." Jumping up from the stool, Aya grabbed her guitar and made for the door. "Thank you ever so much for lunch."

"No, wait," Elleah said, following her through the apartment. "You don't have to go. Stay for a while. Get your feet under you."

Hands gripping her sole possession, she shook her head.

"Well, take this, then," she said, handing Aya a small package. Elleah shook her head. "Just a bit of food and such...and my number. If you run into trouble—"

"Why?"

"We all need someone, dear," Elleah said, reaching tender fingers to hook Aya's hair over her ear. "It's okay to accept help."

Aya hugged her, then fled before the tears overtook her. She had been eighteen years old and had never experienced such kindness.

Her body lurched. Trip shook her back to the present.

"What the bloody hell are you on about?" his voice hissed.

He was capable of so much, yet he had never followed his grandmother's advice and accepted help. Help was not charity.

A nerve fluttered under his left eye, and he jerked her arm again. "You don't know shit."

"Let me go." She pulled free, sure she'd bear the marks of a bruise from his hold. "I know enough to know I'm right."

"The fuck you are."

She shrugged and turned. She had to get away. This didn't help either one of them. "You asked." She started to walk away, praying her legs would hold her. The pain in his eyes shot through her like a knife. Catching the door by the handle, she turned. "I'm not one of your yes-men. Next time you don't really want an answer—don't ask."

For Elleah's sake, she had tried. And failed. Tomorrow, she'd make arrangements to go.

****

What the fuck? Where the hell had she gotten her information? No one... Trip drew a shuddered breath, his mind running through details he strove to forget. The mysterious file that had turned his trial around. Truth be told, the information was all there if anyone bothered to look. That's why he'd been let off so easily. Yet no one in the media had bothered to ask—or report the truth. His manager, Arnold, not wanting to make matters worse and smear Kurt's memory, hadn't offered. Even the cops had taken the scene at face value. No need to delve deeper. He and Kurt were just a batch of bad boys—debauched celebrities. The memory of the warm ooze of his friend's blood had him grip his fists tight. The iron scent of bodily fluids filled his nostrils. Weak tears dripped from the ends of his lashes.

Trip strode into the men's room, confirmed it was empty, and locked the main door. Hands braced flat to the stall wall, he slapped his palm hard against the cool surface. The ping of the metal and sting of the impact did little to numb the pain. He didn't want to think about that night *ever* again. He didn't want to make room for the earth-shattering grief of the loss of his best friend—the utter failure of his every attempt to save Kurt…from himself.

He laid his forehead on the steel frame. The heat of unshed emotion clogged his throat. By what right did this woman have to throw the whole messy scene in his face like an accusation? What he did, he did for the love of a brotherhood—a man closer to him than his own family.

Even today, he didn't understand where it had all gone wrong. Powerless and weak. No matter how he tried to help, every effort had been thwarted, sidetracked, and derailed. It seemed though, in hindsight, the decline of Kurt's mental state had been a gradual progression into the depths of depression. Like slow-cooking a frog. The poor frog didn't even know when the water started to boil. Misery of fame was often overlooked in favor of reputation, influence, attention, and the constant demands of life on the road. At the time, in the midst of chaos, Kurt's melancholy seemed to come overnight. *Blam.* Trip couldn't understand how things had gotten better and better for the band, yet Kurt diminished before his eyes.

If only he could go back in time…

"Whoa, man," Trip had yelled to be heard above the roar of the engine from that fateful night. The road noise was like thunder, while the whistling wind whipped over the convertible sports car. He gripped the door handle as Kurt navigated a hairpin turn. Catching his breath, he called out, "Where we goin'?"

"Who cares?" Kurt shouted, turning his head to look at Trip.

Even in the darkness, Kurt's eyes shone with the lunacy of the moment. A manic glint that made Trip's stomach clench. He knew this stare well. The let's-jump-out-of-a-plane-today sparkle.

Trip had been in this situation far too many times during the last couple of years. The back and forth between them an almost-perfected dance. Something good would happen to offset the slump, and Kurt's more excessive side would kick into overdrive. If he were drinking, he'd drink more. If there were drugs involved, he became experimental. Enough was never enough. Trip participated with a watchful eye, knowing Kurt's tendency to go to the extreme. Predictable in his unpredictable behavior.

On that fateful night, the buzz from the cocaine hit had rocketed Kurt's adrenaline into high gear. Trip went along for a lot of things, but after a near-miss overdose a few years before, he steered clear of the drugs.

"Really, who cares?" Kurt picked up his phone to glance at the texts. "We're on top, man. Finally, on top."

"Eyes on the road, buddy."

Kurt tossed the phone to Trip. The screen filled with congratulatory texts, notifications, and buzz from other social media sites on their recent win for their latest album.

"Gold, baby."

Trip lifted off the seat marginally to put the cell in his pocket and away from Kurt who didn't need further distractions. He glanced through the windshield as the car lost momentum on the steep incline. To his right, the city skyline lit the vista in a twinkling glitter. Los Angeles ever beautiful from a distance, but like their band, so corruption-filled from within.

Then Kurt pulled an ornate flask from between his thighs and drank deeply. Where the hell had that come from? Trip's hands gripped the dashboard.

"How many years to get here?" Kurt held the flask high in the air in salute. "How many? And now we're on top. Top of the charts—world-fucking-wide—"

"World-fucking-wide!" Trip echoed, holding his fist out for a knuckle bump.

Iron Clad—the name of their band, their baby, and brainchild of two youths from entirely different backgrounds, who'd met by chance on the beachfront in California. Kurt worked at the hotel and Trip on extended family holiday, while his mother tried for another marriage. Brought together through their love of music, they had strived for this very moment since they started jamming. But what should have been the highest point of their career seemed riddled by rumors of band break-up, drug busts, and dirty deals.

Trip had tried to keep a lid on things, but the band had had enough. They wanted their fair share, what they deserved. Unfortunately, most of *Iron Clad's* earnings had been squandered away by the one person Trip trusted most. Yet here he sat, still trying to connect. To recapture what they were. Their essence. What made them great. This win, the Grammy, their moment. It belonged to the two of them. The rest of the five-person band could go to hell for all Trip cared. Somehow, he would find a way to bring Kurt back and make him whole again.

The engine roared. Kurt pushed the clutch, rammed the stick into gear, and took the turn on a fishtail.

"Hey." Trip capped the flask and tossed it behind the seats while one hand gripped the door handle. "That was close."

"Not close enough." Kurt banged his hands on the steering wheel. He'd purchased the vehicle yesterday afternoon in anticipation of the awards show. "She's a panther on the hunt," he purred. "Watch her hug the corners, race the wind. She's glorious and free." He circumnavigated the twists of the narrow mountain road, heedless and unaware of anyone else using the near-deserted highway. "We're on top, man, and we've got to go to the highest high to celebrate."

What else could he do? Trip had tried to take the car keys—good luck there. In desperation, he'd jumped in the car to prevent Kurt from driving off alone. Their friendship was a bond, an unspoken oath of solidarity. He raised his fist. "Fucking A."

In the pre-dawn pink of an awakening sky, Trip turned his head toward his lifelong friend. The blue hue from the dash illuminated Kurt from the nose down, casting his eyes in shadow, but Trip knew the crazed glow of the moment—the high that could never be obtained through a drug.

"Together, man. We do this together," Trip shouted.

"You're my best friend," Kurt returned, facing Trip, his voice calm. Despite the noise, Trip heard every word as though they were in the quiet room of a library. "You never forget who we sing our songs for. You keep us moving toward the goals, man."

Then, as fleeting as a falling star, the moment ended. Kurt leaned over the gearshift, the corners of his mouth lifted in a drunken grin.

"You, too…" Trip started, but a flash of movement caught his attention. "Watch out—"

A pair of glowing bullseyes bore down on them. Kurt swerved, fingers light on the wheel, and the panther obeyed. "How's that for handling?" Kurt boasted.

"Oh my God! Too close," Trip yelled. "Slow it down, man. No need to kill the buzz."

"No way, man. I told you, we're going to the top."

Kurt slammed the gears and plunged the gas pedal to the floor. He took the next turn a hair's breadth from the guardrail and twisted the wheels a little too wide to compensate, causing the beast to balk at his demands.

In a moment of clarity as they descended over the cliff face, Trip had realized he and Kurt had been destined for this moment from the beginning. In the end, no amount of optimism would fix what was broken. Nothing could have prevented this fall.

Someone banged on the bathroom door.

Trip opened his eyes and stared blankly at the steel wall of the bathroom stall. He needed a drink—bad.

Chapter Ten

Aya heard the slam of metal, deep mumbling, and the rush of water, followed by the crinkle of a paper towel. A moment later, the lock turned, and Trip opened the door wide.

He held onto the jamb, effectively blocking the entrance. Reddened eyes glowered at her. "Come to gloat?"

The memory of the teenager from the kitchen vivid in her mind, she tried to hold his stare but failed. Dropping her gaze to his feet cased in leather loafers, she shook her head. In no position to throw stones, she'd only walked a few paces when she returned.

A current snapped between them. The hair rose on her arms. Again, she tilted her head to focus on his face. She knew his features so well, and that scared her. The dewdrop of his bottom lip, which had started to curl down just after Kurt's first stint in rehab.

Momentarily giving up on questioning her motives, Aya rolled up on her toes and braced her palms along his smooth cheeks. "You shaved."

Trip opened his mouth, but instead of waiting for words, she tipped his head toward hers and placed her mouth on his. When he didn't pull away, she slipped her tongue through the gap and stroked. He gasped, and under her touch, a tremor ran through him. Her fingers caressed his hair behind his ears as she skimmed her lips across his.

He growled deep in his throat, and his hands gripped her head while the kiss intensified. A hand moving to the small of her back, he folded her to him. She didn't resist. His need for her was thrilling.

At last, she drew away, breathless. Feet flat to the tiles, she looked around, finding herself just inside the bathroom pushed up against the now-closed door. "I didn't want to like you," she said, panting, fingers tracing the lines around his mouth.

His clear gaze, like burnt coal, sizzled. Then the skin to either side of his eyes crinkled, and he snorted. "That's good," he replied, shaking his head. Chuckling, he dropped his hands to her shoulders. "You're not my type, anyway."

Releasing her hold, she allowed her arms to fall to her sides. She couldn't resist the quirk of her lips, and she cocked her head. "A relief, then. We can go about our business."

He wiped a hand across his brow. "Have dinner with me," he said and reached to brush a piece of hair behind her ear.

"No."

"No?"

She smiled and adjusted her clothes. "That's what it means—no."

He leaned close so their noses almost touched. "You're a tough nut to crack."

She lowered her lids and glanced up at him. "Better if you don't try." A flame in her gut caused combustible heat farther down. "I have to get back to work."

An uncertainty colored the irises of his eyes, and she wanted to look away but couldn't. What could he see in the depths of her gaze?

He lifted a hand to curve around the back of his neck and tilted his head. "How do you know so much about me?"

She raised one shoulder. "Everyone knows so much about you. Ask Arnold. I'm no different. Just another groupie."

Was she?

His gaze sharpened, and he shook his head. "I might have thought so last night but not now."

"Why?" The question jumped out. She licked her suddenly dry lips. If only she had the courage to slip back to the restaurant. But that would mean turning around and fumbling to open the door while he stood so close. His gaze seared, and she seemed powerless to move or even try.

His finger crooked under her chin, leveling their gazes. "Because I remember you. You came to see me at the trial—not the exhibit, the spectacle."

"You can't know that," she said, shaking her head, while guilty heat flooded her cheeks.

"Yet I do." His thumb rubbed along her jaw, each stroke a sensation.

The hair on her arms stood at attention from wrist to elbow. She swallowed back a lump, choked with emotion.

She shook her head, lamely trying to free his hold. "I have to get…" Her heart hammered, and her breath became shallow. She snaked her arm behind to grasp the handle. She should have left today. Each hour brought her closer to being exposed. By him or the feds. She didn't know which she now feared more. "They'll wonder where I am."

He nodded. "And I have a show to perform." He sighed. "Still, here we are, so have dinner…"

When she opened her mouth to respond, he leaned in and placed his lips to hers, an echo of her own maneuver. Whisper soft, the kiss held a promise of depth but was feather light, leaving her expectant and dizzy. Then he pulled back. "After your shift—when I'm done with the show."

She blinked several times, nodded, and then said, "No."

Trip laughed, just a small rumble from his chest released through his nostrils. "What time do you get off?"

"I don't stick around." She had the sudden urge to let him know she would be leaving, otherwise, she might be inclined to reveal everything. Like so many others before, if she revealed her true self, he would recoil. "This is only temporary." She flapped a hand to the side. "The whole waitressing thing."

"What a coincidence," he replied. "For me, too. The gig, I mean."

Trip lowered his face to hers and kissed her again. This time, she wanted to turn the lock on the door and push him farther into the bathroom and take him, just one last time before she left. A memory to hold onto. Like the song he'd sung, never knowing it was written for him. A secret memory.

As if reading her mind, he lowered his fingers to the small of her back and brushed his pelvis against hers. He tipped his head and grasped the lobe of her ear between his teeth. She arched her neck, granting better access. As he moved his lips along her collarbone, she moaned.

Then the door pushed from the other side before slapping back against the casing.

"What?" came an impatient voice. "Is someone in there?"

Trip backed away and coughed. "Just a minute." He pushed a hand to the middle of the door.

"Fuck," she mumbled under her breath. "That's all I need, to be seen by a customer coming out of the men's room."

"Who's in there?" The man's sharp reply served to douse the flames of moments before. He sounded cranky.

"Here, here," Trip whispered, retaining his position, palm flat to the door while he pointed to a stall.

Aya nodded and entered the cubicle. She cupped her burning cheeks, trying to control her breathing.

The main door squeaked, and heavy footfalls stamped inside. "What is going on in here?" The indignant voice echoed off the tiled walls. Then a shuffling before he said, "Oh, oh, you're…you're…"

"I really should be in my own dressing room," Trip replied. His voice smooth, polished—the star performer. "But I was about to go on and just needed a place to breathe before the show. You know how it is."

Aya doubted the man would know how it was to be an internationally acclaimed entertainer.

"Oh, yes. Of course." The man stumbled over his words. "So sorry to intrude, but…I have to…is there perhaps…?"

"No, no. I wouldn't hear of it," Trip said. "Please accept my apologies. I am fine now."

Aya waited to hear Trip leave. The squeak of the

main door followed the closing of the stall next to hers and signaled her opening. Hating that he managed to exit without incident and she was left to fend for herself, open to exposure the moment she moved through the room. She gripped her stomach, fluffed her hair, scanned her clothing, and took a deep breath. Opening the stall door, she slipped out, holding her breath as she moved into the hallway after checking right and then left before emerging fully.

Just as she was about to release of a sigh of relief, Trip grabbed her upper arm.

"Oh." She placed her hands on her hips and bent forward. "You scared me."

"Dinner, then."

She'd dug herself a hole. Seeing no way out at the moment when her brain refused to function, she nodded.

On shaky legs, Aya strode back though the archway and into the lounge. She had to *leave*. Now.

Chapter Eleven

More comfortable than he'd been in a long time, Trip took to the stage and gave the best performance of the last year—maybe longer. The ovation provided a salve. Perhaps, he really could move on.

Arnold rushed to pat him on the shoulder. "Well done," he said. "There's the star I can market."

While Arnold yammered about next steps and phases, Trip scanned the restaurant for her, annoyed he still didn't know her name. Guests stood and shook his hand as he walked by, an action that hadn't happened in a very long time.

"You're back, baby," Arnold said, walking with Trip to the dingy dressing room.

Once there, Arnold had Trip autograph headshots taken before the accident. Headshots featuring unscarred cheeks and forehead. He paused to study the face. Who was the man glaring back with mock attitude? "Someone ignorant to the ways of the world," he said, finishing the stack and laying them to the side.

"What's that?"

Unaware he had spoken aloud, Trip glanced up at his manager. "Oh, nothing. I think we'll need new photos done."

Arnold um-hummed, pulled out his phone, and made notes.

Restless, Trip left the dressing room and scanned

the lounge again. No sign of her. "Damn it."

Not that it was unusual for him not to know the name of a woman he'd had sex with, though knowing her name would be most convenient now. A momentary chagrin flamed his veins at the amount of times that had happened, but he *wanted* to know *her* name. That was the difference.

Leaning against the door jamb to the side of the stage, he scoped the lounge to identify someone he could ask. First, he'd have to devise an excuse on why he wanted to know so not to draw attention. His gaze drifted to the bar and the neat rows of decorative bottles filled with various liquors. He licked his lips, imagining the flavors, and as he did, he tasted the honey-sweet residual of the woman's lip balm left from their last kiss. But after his behavior with her the other night at the bar, he couldn't ask Mark.

Or could he?

Determined, Trip strode across the room.

Arnold intercepted him before he could gain the bartender's eye. His manager coughed before speaking. The rumble rippled through the handlebar moustache. "Worked up a thirst, did you?"

Trip's gaze roamed between Arnold's all-encompassing walrus moustache and the hippy-chic bartender now waiting for Trip's order. Sober, he found himself hyper-alert to his manager's tone. His plan of getting the woman's name on the quiet had already failed before he even tried.

Instead of answering Arnold directly or offering a reaction to the insinuation, Trip nodded and drew broadside to the thick mahogany bar. "Water, no ice, lemon wedge."

Surprise widened the young man's tanned face as Trip held his doe-brown gaze. Pleasure at the stain of color highlighting Mark's cheekbones fostered his courage to actually drink the water while he wished for vodka with the same lemon wedge. He fisted his hand to steady his fingers and ease the tremor before grasping the glass. Gulping the contents, he smothered a belch before lending his attention back to Arnold.

The manager sighed. "This gig is getting better and better." He gestured with his chin back to the room at large.

Trip shrugged, unsure whether to take the comment as a question or a statement. He rolled the cuffs of his shirt to his elbows as a stall tactic while he tried to figure out how to resume his plan of finding out the woman's name and where she was. Based on the last couple of nights, he assumed her shift ended after his set, not before.

"The crowd really responded tonight," Arnold continued. "A bit touch-and-go there for a while, wouldn't you say?"

"How so?" Trip searched the faces in the room, sure she'd be there. Perhaps in the kitchen. If he could avoid Reggie, or that great giant blond, the surly chef, he'd charm one of the other wait staff into giving him her name.

"Never mind." Arnold shook his head, and the moustache wobbled comically. "It's been a nice rest and recuperation being here. The island is…quaint. I know you like being close to your sister and such, but it's time to start planning. Getting *Iron Clad* back together will take a bit of doing, but we can hit the road…"

"The road?" His heart slammed against his chest, and a cold sweat dripped down his spine. Trip didn't know if they, meaning he, was ready for that yet. Performing to small, intimate crowds was one thing. Stadiums, however, even if they could get the bookings, were different.

Arnold's blood-shot eyes dashed everywhere but refused to focus on Trip. He coughed again, a sure sign of anxiety. "But...never mind that now. We need...need...exposure."

Trip lodged his hands in his pockets. The tremble started the moment Arnold's tone took on that familiar note of business, and his face pinched stubbornly. Trip knew what was coming. Time's up. But he wasn't ready. No way.

Trip opened his mouth to speak, but the words lodged in his throat while Arnold continued his staggered speech.

"Bills past due. Demands on the corporation. The legal beagles needing their pound of flesh for not only the court time but the change in corporate structure. You're no longer a partnership, and we have to look at the solo career. We can't survive on what was... We need to move forward—with a plan..."

Arnold pulled a wheezed breath. The cigarettes peeked out of his breast pocket, and Trip could almost smell the man's need for a drag in the same manner he, himself, itched for liquor.

The shiver snaked up Trip's arm and threatened to take over his whole body. "No," he managed at last.

"On Tour."

Their words clashed midair, and silence between them followed.

Arnold laid his palm flat on the polished wood and bent close to Trip. "Enough with the kid gloves. Months have passed. You've tried the new material, and it's working. Time to pull on the big-boy undies. Playboy freewheeler works for a while but not anymore. It doesn't pay the bills. You're good with the numbers, so you look. Tell me how we're going to continue to pay everyone…for…doing…nothing."

Each enunciated word landed like a blow. Lips pulled back, Arnold's teeth bared in the midst of all the facial fur provided a monstrous flare. All the confidence from an hour ago vanished.

"While you continue to stagger around feeling sorry for yourself, some of us have had to hold everything together. Enough. Make a decision. You're either in, or you're out." Arnold slapped the wood, and the reverberation matched the quiver in Trip's hands as he kept them stowed away in his pockets.

When Trip didn't respond, Arnold raised his hand from the table top with a flick of his wrist toward Trip's face. "Fine."

Trip locked his knees to remain standing. "Fine," he said to his manager's retreating back. Like an anchor, Trip pulled everyone down with him. He knew how he'd gotten here, yet was powerless to change. For a moment, however brief, she had made him feel life again was possible, but she had disappeared, too. Arnold's cold splash of realism rectified his ineffectualness.

Arnold proved right on one point. Everyone had to live their own lives. Stop relying on him. He couldn't carry the load. Not alone. Not without Kurt.

Trip pulled his hands from his pockets, smashed

them together with a thunderclap of sound, and turned to the bartender. "Enough pretending," he said, a slight sneer coloring his words. "Vodka. Rocks. Fuck the lemon."

****

Aya left the building. She did. Determination set, feigning illness, she'd asked Ronaldo, the chef, if she could cut out early. He'd stuck his head out into the dining room, scanned the patrons, and nodded. It had been a slow night, anyway.

Yet like a yo-yo on a string, she bounced back and forth in indecision.

She wound her way through the resort corridors, across the foyer, nodding to the front desk staff until she exited to the beach area. Her gait slowed along the boardwalk, the distance between her and *him* not overly far. If she listened closely, she could hear the strains from the piano. They blended with the rhythm set from the breaking waves.

Farther along, the great expanse gapped black, except where the beach sparkled with equally placed lampposts. Out to sea, the occasional boat, lit from bow to stern, bobbed across the horizon under the blanket of stars. Just a short walk, two turns, and she'd be at her flat. There she'd pack what few belongings she had and be done.

Aya brushed her palms together.

Was this really what she wanted? Uncertainty swirled around in her brain, and confusion weighed against her heart. The mixture, like a toxin, slowed her step and labored her breathing. Finally, she threw her hands in the air and slumped down on a bench to watch people pass, walking their dogs or strolling with their lovers or children. None of them seemed to have a care in the world while she, burdened with events of the past, had staged her life to flee from caring or any emotional involvement.

Elleah's words, spoken so long ago, rang in her memory as though the woman were sitting next to her. "Everyone needs help now and again."

My God, how had she let this happen? She knew better. This infatuation had nothing to do with help. Trip wasn't just some guy, not just another artist, a fling she could set aside. He offered the link to all she wanted, and all she could be. She saw her potential. He brought out the best of her.

And he *moved* her. He awoke something long since dormant. A caring...compassion. She closed her eyes, and the sad tilt to his eyes assaulted her memories. The hopeful spark when he took her in his arms.

A dragonfly zoomed in close to her hand where it rested on her knee, rose up to hover, and then parked on top. Rather than flick the small beast away, Aya watched the light from the lamppost reflect on its majestic wings. The stillness of the insect made it look as though it were fake. She tilted so her upper torso closed the gap and blew softly toward the vibrant blue form. Instantly, the wings flickered, and it rose then settled again, resuming its spot.

The dragonfly should be scared. She could kill it. Wasn't that what people did to pesky insects? Yet he remained still, trusting her not to injure. "Oh, my little friend," Aya said softly. "I could easily pull your fragile wings from your body, and you'd never fly again."

"But you won't."

Aya started, heart pounding, and twisted in her

seat. Her hands flew to her heart where it pumped wildly under her fingers. The noxious thick flow of her blood let loose like a dam flooding a river. Spots formed, and dizziness made her lightheaded.

Hands braced along the back of the bench, Trip angled his body above hers. He straightened. "There he goes." He pointed into the darkness.

Aya followed his line of sight, the black of the night obscuring her view of the departed dragonfly.

Trip rounded the bench and flopped down beside her. His shoulder nudged hers. "You wouldn't, right?"

"Wouldn't what?"

His chin lifted to where the fly had departed. "Rip off the little wings. Be a shame for him to never fly again. That's what he was meant to do."

The double meaning wasn't lost on her. She couldn't help herself and laughed. "Maybe."

"I don't believe you."

"That's up to you." She sat back and listened to the sounds of the night, her heart resuming a fluttering beat. Music, people, ocean, traffic—all around them but not invading their space. Amongst all of it, they were alone, isolated in their small universe as defined by the length of the bench, intimate. "I can't alter what people believe. I learned that a long time ago."

Air whistled past his lips. "Harsh." He leaned forward so his elbows rested on his thighs, and his hands dangled between his legs. He lowered his head and cocked it to the side. "And to think I left a perfectly excellent vodka in the hopes that you could change my mind on the state of my world."

Again, Aya laughed. She alter someone's view on the world? Absurd. She who had never been accepted because of her name and what her grandfather did decades ago? Condemned for acts not her own. A giggle bubbled, and she guffawed. Misery and the general belief all people would "get you in the end" had ruled her life for as long as she could remember. Social interaction had become simply a means of starting the countdown to exposure and ridicule. A snort erupted, and she covered her face. Still, she giggled. Her sides hurt, and she braced a palm against her ribcage. The conversation was not really hilarious, but she couldn't help herself.

"It's not that funny," Trip said, turning in his seat and watching her with open incredulity.

Sure, he likely considered her slightly unhinged by this point, but if he ever learned she had been studying him for months—years really, since being taken in by his grandmother—and followed him here, he'd peg her as unstable and report her to the police before the feds even had a chance to find her. She had to go.

She had tired of her internal monologue.

Shadows played with his features, sharpening his cheeks and softening his eyes. He looked kind. She could almost believe it…but she knew better. "What's funny is me sitting here with you," she said at last and gained her feet, brushing moisture from her eyes. "It's fucking hysterical that I haven't left yet."

"Let me walk you home."

"Are you kidding me?" She raised a palm to halt his rise. "Trip Vincent walk me home? You're not Reginald, and this isn't the 1950s when your grandmother performed here. I'm fine."

Chapter Twelve

"Wait. What? How'd you—never mind." He shook his head. "Aya, wait." Trip stood as soon as she turned to walk away. The sound of her name on his lips felt right. Simple, yet foreign—unusual, like the woman he wanted to know on a deeper level.

She couldn't know what it had cost him to not one-shot that vodka. How he'd twisted the crystal glass this way and that, catching the light, working up the nerve to ask Mark her name. She couldn't know the thrill in spotting her so soon after leaving the lounge. Her sitting so close was a gift—a sign? Or that spark of hope the mere sight of her generated.

He couldn't let her go. Some instinct told him if he let her go, she'd be gone. He drew breath. "You promised me dinner."

"What?" She whirled around, her small trim body taut. "Are you serious? No." The words tumbled over one another.

Catching up to stand beside her, he pouted his lips and tilted his head. "But you promised." Completing the pose, he held his hands together, prayer-style. "A promise is a promise."

Her hands fisted on her hips. "You're not five."

"So my manager reminded me today."

"Then listen to him. Arnold knows what he's about."

"Hey." Trip reached out to grasp her arm before she could swing away again. "How do you know my manager?" He glanced down at the wooden walkway, then back into her eyes. "My grandparents? The details of my trial…"

For a moment, her face blanked. Then her straight brows pinched above a pert nose. A line creased in the middle. She drew her bottom lip between her teeth, then released it with a huff. "I read."

Did it matter? He decided to let it go as unimportant. He didn't want to be distracted, reasoning the information wasn't hard to find out. "I guess," he said. "Still, you did promise."

Her brow retained the wrinkle of puzzlement, though her mouth lifted. She cocked her head. "I wouldn't say I promised."

"I took your word as a promise."

When she semi-turned again, less brisk, he followed and fell into step with her. For someone so tiny, she had a long stride. They walked in silence, their progress easy on the worn planks of the boardwalk.

His sister's place could be seen from where they were, but he didn't know when the rest of his family would arrive. He didn't think he could slip in unnoticed, especially with Aya in tow. They passed the A-frame beach house without comment. He glanced through the cheery windows to see people gathered in Evangeline's living room. His cousin Wendee with her man, Toby, clearly visible, casual and at ease on the window seat. Others formed shadows in the background. His heart lurched in lonely longing to be embraced by his family. Guilt and embarrassment over how far he'd fallen stabbed him. Eva didn't deserve the side of him he'd shown her all these months. With a nod toward the beach house, he made an internal commitment to do better by her.

He caught Aya glancing through to the people outlined in shadow in the cottage. "A person's word should always be their promise," she said.

Trip started, and his step fumbled. They'd walked so far without a word, lost in thought and surrounded by the chatter of birds and night noises, that her statement took him by surprise.

She glanced up at him and reached out a hand, though she didn't touch him. "You okay?"

He scanned the front of the house for signs that anyone had noticed him on his way past. "Oh...yeah," he said. "Just focused in my own head."

"Be careful with that. It can be a dangerous occupation."

Trip studied her face. She smiled, her face transformed, somehow younger, and he chuckled, delighted to be in the moment with her. "If you only knew how dangerous."

"I'll bet," she shot back.

They took the stairs up to the road, made their way along Ocean Boulevard until they came to a small café.

"This is where you want to go for dinner?"

She glanced up at him, surprise rounding her eyes, and shook her head. "No." The perplexity of her look accused him of being a moron for asking. She led him around the side of the building, then held up a palm. "Wait here a sec."

She moved in and out of shadow until she stood under a pool of yellow light. Within moments, she returned, sporting jeans and a leather jacket. His breath hitched. She exuded sexy in a hands-off-or-I'll-take-you-down kinda way. A dangerous glint sparkled in her eyes, dark in silhouette, and his body responded. He ran his palms along his jean-clad legs. The urge to take her in that moment engulfed him, and he shook his head to dislodge the compulsion and focus.

She pulled a set of keys from her pocket and proceeded to a nearby shed. They tinkled like sleigh bells. "The owners let me store my bike in here. Damned sight more convenient than the last place, I'll tell you."

When she rolled the motorcycle down the small ramp, all he could do was whistle. Not just any motorcycle—a classic red Indian, authentic colors, graceful lines, and full of power. Her reference to a "bike" made him first think bicycle, and then perhaps a small moped scooter or some such thing. Never had he expected the exquisite piece of craftsmanship she balanced on the kickstand.

"Here," she said and handed him a silver-black helmet.

No way could she handle such a bike. Surely, her feet wouldn't even touch the ground.

As the words formed, she zipped her jacket to her chin, donned her own helmet, and tossed a leg over the saddle. She glanced behind her. "You coming?"

Trip didn't think she knew she was tiny. Confidence rolled off her in waves. Arms squared, she appeared as one with the bike. In moments, they glided through the quiet streets, by the marina, until they came to the Coronado Bridge. Here she opened the throttle and shot over the expanse like a bird in flight. Trip quickly moved his hands from where they had rested on his knees to secure around her hips. Soon, they had skirted San Diego and zoomed along the highway— Mexico bound. The ocean to one side and orchards to the other. The moon glinted off the water, and the power of the machine echoed through her hips and up to his arms.

Given the opportunity, he'd have her pull over on the darkened highway, turn in her seat, and straddle him. The power of the machine, combined with her nearness, made him as hard as the asphalt.

She swerved and took each bend in the road as a master. No doubt, she understood the machine's limits. He never experienced the out-of-control blitz like he had as a passenger with Kurt. They travelled fast but not reckless. The wind whipped, and Trip released one of his hands to catch the airstream between his fingers. Freedom enveloped him with an intoxication better than booze. Melody shot through him, and he had the urge to write the lyrics. He hummed, lost to the moment and the gift she'd given him. He didn't notice they had slowed until she turned into a near-vacant parking lot.

He dismounted. "You can ride."

She removed her helmet, fluffing her short hair. Her wide smile brought him a sense of contentment.

"I can."

"I shouldn't be surprised."

She cocked her head. "Why?"

"Because everything about you is a surprise."

She unzipped her jacket and pocketed the keys. "That's because you don't know me."

"I'd like to," he said. Trip had never before expressed an interest in another like Aya. He ran his gaze over her slight form. From the first glance, she'd appeared nothing special, yet she sparked something in him. A mystery. He stepped forward to place the helmet next to hers where she locked them on the back of the seat.

One brow rose. "Trust me…you're better off."

"I'd like to be the judge of that."

She stood and scrutinized him a moment too long. Then she moved away toward the rickety shack. "Let's eat. I'm hungry."

"I'm hungry, too, but I'm not sure it's food I'm after."

She held out her hand, and feeling like he had done this a million times with her, he laced his fingers with hers. Then they walked into what Trip would have termed a hole-in-the-wall joint had there been a wall—or other buildings, for that matter. Instead, the building sat like a bruise on a barren section of highway. A biker's hangout? Maybe. True, there were perhaps a handful of bikes, but it was midweek and late—hard to tell. That the place was open at all proved shocking, never mind it being an establishment fit for food consumption.

Aya released his hand and strode to the counter like she owned it.

"Rosie, my dove." A bearded man, with tattoo sleeves and a foreign accent, came around the bar and embraced her. "I wasn't expecting you. We're almost closed."

Rosie?

Aya smiled easily, looking very much at home. Like a chameleon, she had morphed into someone belonging to the environment. Windblown from the road, casual biker clothing, hand hanging out of her pocket, she fit like the worn leather stools.

"I took a chance. Brought a friend." She cast a glance at Trip, her thumb pointing. "I doubt he's ever had food like yours, Juan."

Trip scoped the joint, taking in the bulky forms in the gloom—a couple still at the bar, heads hanging low, and the woman staring intently from the swinging half doors to the kitchen. He had to agree. Even when they first started out as a band, they hadn't even played such a place. There were dives, and then there was this place.

To make conversation and not piss the man off, Trip leaned an elbow on the counter, aware of the sticky mess now clinging to his shirt, and asked, "What's the house special?"

Juan barely acknowledged Trip before returning his focus to Aya. "For you, your favorite. Dill pickle soup and watermelon salad."

Trip gulped. At any moment, she would reveal the joke—right? Any hunger he may have had evaporated with the mention of dill pickle and soup as one item. He raised a palm from the oak counter. "I'm good, thanks."

Aya patted his hand down. "You're an angel, Juan. Sounds delicious. And I *did* promise my friend dinner."

Payback? Still, how did she even know a place like this existed? Never mind be comfortable holding a conversation.

"No guitar." Juan pointed a beefy finger. "You sing tonight, my Rosie dove."

She looked around and shook her head. "Not much of a crowd. No, not tonight. Just dinner—"

"You sing?" Trip's brows rose.

"As you wish," Juan said.

Aya led Trip to a table with two mismatched

chairs. He wiped his palms on his jeans, felt the wobble of uneven stool legs, and sat hesitantly.

"Below your standards?" Her wide grin stretched ear to ear. Previously unnoticed dimples appeared below her cheekbones.

"You're enjoying this?" He couldn't hold his own smile back. The smell of booze, with a slight hint of tobacco and must, permeated the air. The sturdy table, decorated with rings of brown, had seen its fair share of use. *Burn the place down and start from scratch.* He traced a dark circle with his index finger. For the first time since his teen years, Trip sat uncertain, awkward in a woman's company, at a loss for what to say or do. "You sing?"

"Not really." She shrugged. "You don't have to be good to be a hit in a place like this. Just willing."

"But you sing? What?"

She draped an arm over the rest of her chair and fluttered her fingers in the air. "As though anyone would consider what I do singing compared to the great Trip Vincent."

"Come on," he replied. "What?"

Her movements stalled, and she lowered her gaze. Her tongue swept across her lips before she replied. "This and that. I found this place on my way to the island."

"Bit of a detour."

She laughed. "I guess. I was—perhaps still am, I don't know—chasing something. I didn't quite understand. I just had the urge to go to the island but…" Her stare bore into his. "Came here first."

"Here?" He gaped, then closed his lips and looked around. "I can see the attraction."

"Come on." She glanced around and nodded.

"Seriously, this was the best you could do?"

She laughed. "I didn't specifically pick this place." Aya sat forward, and the table tipped precariously. "I just didn't know if I—if I…should go on. So here I stopped to re-evaluate my motives and determine whether to go on as planned."

Trip lifted a hand in a circular fashion to encourage her to continue.

"Not a matter of the best I could do. I just stopped for the night. Had to rethink my plan—not that I had much of one. Juan's a great guy…a little scary to look at, I'll grant you, but nice."

Trip glanced over his shoulder. The woman with the lanky platinum hair and thick line of black roots had moved to the bar and continued to drill bullets through them with her beady eyes. "I bet."

She flapped her fingers again. "Never mind your judgment. I've seen worse."

The thought of her being in worse dives than this plagued him for a moment. Sure, she made like she could handle her own. Obviously she could. Still, he didn't want her to have to. He longed to reach an arm over her shoulders and reassure her she didn't have to face these things alone. Then he stopped. He didn't want to be alone.

A long moment passed while they listened to the jukebox. "Go on," he said finally. "How did stopping at a place like this cement your idea to continue on to the island?"

"I had my guitar on my back when I came in, and Juan demanded I sing for my food."

"And you did." Trip laughed outright. "Come on.

That doesn't happen."

Juan signaled from the bar. "Chow's up."

She shrugged and stood. "Believe what you will." She set the dishes in the middle of the table. The combination of smells, fresh and foreign yet familiar, blended with the aroma of hard liquor, and his stomach gurgled.

"Doesn't matter," she said and picked up her spoon. "The food was worth it, and the audience grateful."

Resisting the urge to clean his spoon on his shirt, he dipped it into the greenish sludge.

Aya closed her eyes as she sipped from the utensil, seeming to enjoy the contents. When she didn't fall to the sticky floor poisoned, he followed her lead. The heady blend of dill, cheddar, and spice assaulted and awoke his taste buds.

"Umm," he murmured. "This…came out of there." He tilted his chin back toward the kitchen.

She nodded, angling the bowl to gather the last bits with her spoon.

Juan set two mugs of beer on the table and grunted. The froth splashed over the side.

Aya watched him return to the bar.

Trip reached a hand to cover hers. "So was it worth it? Did you make the right choice?"

She stared at him a long while, fork poised over the salad. "Yes."

Chapter Thirteen

Had she known all along? Likely. Aya knew what she wanted. Yet the prospect seemed impossible. Unattainable. Logically, any relationship she had with him couldn't last. Once he found out about her, everything would end. Still, following her heart, here she sat next to the man she knew she loved.

In her tiny flat, they made love. Road hot and filled with the passion of freedom, they came together like opposing winds in a hurricane, meshing—fusing—igniting. He entered her like a pagan god, and she rode him, giving thrust for thrust. Later, slick with sweat, windows open to the sea breeze fluttering the curtains, they turned to one another in tenderness. Then they learned about each other's bodies. Sated the need and satisfied the wants. Thrilled in the knowledge and giggled in the closeness.

Trip's fingers traced her bare arms. "You are the most beautiful thing."

She lay curled next to his body, her head in the nook between neck and shoulder. Her palm lay atop the springy mass of chest hair. "You're not so bad."

The musk of their sweat and mutual climax made her yearn for him to fill her again and again. She rolled on top, hovering above him. With her moist vagina, she stroked his penis, feeling it grow between her legs.

"You're a wanton little thing." His voice graveled.

She drew his bottom lip into her mouth, sliding her tongue along the contours, while stroking his engorged member in the same fluid fashion.

He moaned, hands on her hips, pushing her toward the tip for entry, but she held firm on her knees. She stroked back and forth.

He reared up, repositioned his palms to either side of her head, and kissed her deeply.

She caressed his tongue with her own, pulling it deep into her mouth, releasing it gently only to pull it back again.

His hands took the weight of her breasts, thumbs stroking the nipples where they pebbled under his touch.

"You're playing with fire," he said, head landing back on the pillow while his hands molded to her hips.

"I know."

****

They had spent the night in her tiny apartment, barely sleeping, until the dawn began to crest the horizon. Aya rolled over, content and sore in places long neglected, if ever used to their full potential, to see a smiling, goofy-faced Trip with fresh coffee and baked croissants from the café downstairs. After, they made love in the shower, and she giggled like a school girl, slippery with suds and bursting with passion. Sex had never been this way before for her. Would it last?

For today, this moment, with this man, she wouldn't worry about discovery. Wouldn't worry about the family legacy of shame. Nor Trip's reaction. For now, she would gift herself an accumulation of memories to see her through.

Trip filled the hole that had echoed a cry of

yearning unheard for ages. She had learned to ignore it. The sudden silence of her hungry heart terrified her for the ramifications when the dream ended—as she knew it would. She shook her head to rid the dreaded reality. But in the moment, the depths of Trip's gray-green eyes mirrored her own need, and she was powerless to walk away.

Now, midafternoon, she foolishly sat beside him out in the open. Her feet dangled over the edge of the Del's outdoor pool, enjoying the sun on her back, and the man she could lose herself to at her side. The ten-foot walls, live with creeping vines and fragrant flowers, provided privacy from the general public, though the pool was open to the hotel guests. Despite his celebrity, Trip seemed unaffected by the many sidelong glances cast his way. But no one approached. Seemed the paparazzi interest in Trip had dwindled in the months since the court verdict. Purposely shunning the tension in her shoulders and habitual dread, Aya allowed herself to feel somewhat insulated in discovery through some published photograph.

Someone like her being seen with a rock star would certainly draw the notice of the feds. "The hell with it," she muttered.

Trip's hand lightly touched her own. "What?" His smile added warmth to the bright day.

She glanced down at his long, tapered fingers laced in her own. He was someone destined for the finer things in life. Where would someone like her ever fit? She raised her eyes to meet his. Lines crinkled the edges, visible to the side of his trendy sunglasses. He appeared more relaxed than she had ever seen him as his foot splashed up and down in the water populated by children.

"Umm, what?" she asked, leaning so her shoulder touched his and their feet met below the water's surface. Their toes tickled one another.

"You said something."

"No." Her toes stroked the bottom of his foot.

He laughed and shrugged, then kissed her temple. "Okay." He pulled back a moment before he leaned in and laid his lips against hers. A hand cupped the back of her neck, and he drew her close and deepened the kiss. Sighing, he rubbed her nose with the tip of his. "Hungry?"

Breathless, she smiled. "Yes."

His thumb traced the contours of her skull, and he chuckled. "For food."

"I could use a drink."

In one fluid motion, he popped up from the side of the pool. "I'll be right back."

"I'll be here." She nodded, then pointed to their chairs. "Or right there."

He laughed and strode off. Aya let the tension flow away. She leaned back on her elbows and enjoyed the view. Trip didn't look as skinny and unhealthy as he had when she'd first seen him. Today, he was lithe, lean, vibrant, and full of everything she wanted to share.

Something caught her attention. She sat up, her ears perked. Children laughed and played all around. Parents shouted, blending in a cacophony of noise, yet a plopping sound made her search the shallow water around her feet. A small kid had jumped into the water close by. Aya picked up her towel and glanced around for the parents. The pool was busy but not crowded.

Judging by his swimmers, the little boy was perhaps three, and he hadn't surfaced. No lifejacket or floatation of any kind adorned his little body. He didn't struggle. No tossing of his head. His hands pawed the water, but his head remained below. She stood to stare down into the clear water.

Bubbles drifted from the boy's open mouth, and fingers clawed at the liquid. Unable to gain purchase, his feet remained planted on the pool bottom. Aya knelt down to get a better look. Time stood still. Where were the parents? Who was in charge of this youngster?

His lack of panic kept her calm. He'd been under long enough that she knew she couldn't hold her breath that long, and the bubbles had ceased to emerge.

Reality finally hit. "Oh my God." She breathed deeply and rolled into the water, grabbed the little body, and hauled him to the surface.

He was so small her hands wrapped easily around his waist. Breaking the surface, his head rested against her shoulder, and she patted his back. He coughed, sputtered, and his hands wound around her neck. His heart thumped against her own like a racing rabbit. But he didn't cry.

"Hey," she soothed. "It's okay. It's okay, little guy. You'll be fine now."

Aya moved to the edge of the pool and sat him down on the side, keeping her face close to his. When he stopped coughing, she asked, "What's your name?" Was he even old enough to talk?

He shook his head and lodged a thumb between his lips. She glanced around. Still, no one raced over. Where were the parents? Anyone? Surely, someone would miss him soon. Even the lifeguards seemed unaware that she had just saved this boy from drowning. The thought caused a shiver to race along her spine and pissed her off at how close this child had come to death. She cupped her palm along his cheek. "Are you okay?"

He nodded and continued to suck his thumb, but his other hand came out of his lap and cupped her cheek, mirroring her own motion.

Aya smiled. "Charmer."

"What's going on?" Trip asked, kneeling down next to the little boy but directing his gaze at her.

"He jumped in," she replied. In a delayed reaction, her stomach rolled and pinched. "I don't know where his parents are. God, Trip, it happened so fast. He didn't have any floaties or anything." She glanced quickly back at the boy, aware her voice had taken a turn, and made an effort to regain her calm. His hand remained in her own. "We have to find his folks."

"For sure. We'll take him over to the towel barn. They'll have someone there to help," he said, set their drinks down next to their chairs, and returned to reach for the boy. The little guy offered no resistance when Trip hoisted him into his arms. "You have a name?"

Aya hopped out of the pool to stand next to Trip. Turning to gather their towels, she became aware of the quiet. Music continued in the background, but the general hum of the crowd had died. She spun round, and her heart dropped. Camera phones were poised at the ready or already clicking away.

Then a woman came flying through the crowd. "Jamie!"

Trip turned toward the yell.

"Jamie."

The little boy's thumb popped out of his mouth, and his arm lifted from Trip as he pivoted, drawn to the voice.

The woman grabbed him close and spun in a wide circle before directing her focus on Trip. "We were just over there for ice cream. Next thing you know, I turn around, and he's gone."

A semi-circle had formed around them, and panic gripped Aya. Sweat trickled down her face, mixing in the rivulets of chlorinated water. She searched the area. How could she slip away unnoticed in the gathering throng?

"You're all wet, Jamie," the mother announced to the boy, then lifted her gaze to Trip. "What happened? He can't swim."

Trip pointed to the pool. "He fell in the water, and my friend pulled him to safety."

A low hum danced through the crowd. Aya spun to march away, but Trip grabbed her elbow. "Here's the hero," he announced. A wide grin split his face, and he winked.

Here stood the celebrity working the crowd. He thought she'd be like any of his other cohorts and enjoy the accolades.

She shook her head and leaned close to his ear, trying to keep her face away from the raised camera phones. "I have to go."

He seemed not to hear and didn't release the light grip on her elbow. "He fell into the pool, and she acted right away to bring him up. We were just on our way to find you," Trip said to the mother.

"Imagine." She hugged the boy to her and brushed a hand along his arm. "Trip Vincent rescued my son."

Aya pulled out of his grip and walked as quickly as she could, head down, for the bathroom. The last thing she heard as she rounded the corner was Trip's announcement of a beach concert.

Chapter Fourteen

Trip sat on a bench along the boardwalk. The wind scuttled the clouds across the horizon. The weather had changed with the mood of the day. The smell of rain filled the air.

Elbows on knees, his head in his hands, he puzzled over what had gone wrong. When? Where? He rubbed his temples, squeezing his forehead. One moment, they'd been awash in the praise of the crowd, and then...Aya disappeared. Just like that. Gone.

Caught up in the adoration, he hadn't noticed her go straight away. He meant to go after her, but... Then Arnold sidetracked him, having caught a social media feed of the concert announcement.

He peeked through the split in his fingers. The tide had begun to break. The swell noisy as it hit the beach.

Speed of light, hell, nothing beat the power of the web.

"You mean it?" Arnold had grabbed him by the shoulders. A positive inflection to the older man's voice Trip hadn't heard in a long time. Even his moustache wobbled happily. "Look at you." He shook Trip a little, nodding. "Just like your old self."

Trip didn't want to be his "old self." He wanted to be the confident, complete man he was with Aya.

Arnold's sausage-like fingers gripped tightly, maneuvering Trip away from the crowd where he leaned his head near Trip's ear. "The timing couldn't be better." He waggled a finger, his voice taking on a conspiratorial air. "I spoke to your cousin, Wendee. Great to have the family connection, I tell you. Managed to arrange everything with the hotel. We're all set. No problem there at all."

Trip took a final scan of the pool area before leaving. What had he done wrong?

Distracted, he nodded in time to the inflection of Arnold's voice. "Yeah, my cousin."

"Sweet. I forget sometimes how deep your roots are planted in the ground around here." They moved into the garden, meandering through the rock path. "Suffice to say, we have a concert to plan."

Trip stopped. He couldn't just leave. He lifted an arm and semi-turned. "But Aya," Trip muttered, stopping mid-stride to circle out of Arnold's grip and scan the area. "Where'd she go?"

Arnold laughed, a deep rumble, and replaced his arm across Trip's shoulders, the weight bearing him down while he propelled Trip forward. "Your friend." The manager's lips puckered. "That's a bit of a gem."

Dread coiled in Trip's stomach. "What?"

Arnold seemed unaware he had spoken. He resumed a determined step. Navigating the garden, they turned in the direction of the beach and strode along the boardwalk. "Don't worry about the young miss. Aya, you say? Strange name. Still, she'll enjoy her day in the press." Reaching into his pocket, he lifted his phone and showed Trip the screen lit with the many pictures circulating of Aya in her bathing suit.

For the first time, Trip noticed her pained expression. The wide eyes and pale features, lips firmed to a solid line. The fear clearly etched in strain lines around her mouth and pinched brows. How could he have missed that?

Simple answer, he'd been caught up in the sea of smiling faces, relieved to find himself in fan favor after so long. Did what they think mean so much to him?

Trip stopped, and Arnold dropped his arm. "I'm that shallow," Trip muttered.

"Umm, what?" Arnold asked, and Trip realized he'd not only spoken aloud, but the man hadn't stopped yammering about the upcoming concert plans.

A tightening, like a band wound round his chest, squeezed. He lifted a hand to his brow. A confused fog muted everything. "Where'd she go?"

"How would I know?" Arnold lifted his palms to the sky, bristly brows arched in the wrinkles leading to his hairline. Then he nodded. "She's a leg up over the others. Won the lottery, that one. Aya? Unique. Yeah, that will play nice. Like I said, she'll have her day in the sun. She'll love it. They all do."

This only served to further crush the air from his lungs. Trip shook his head. "No," he said, taking the phone from Arnold and cupping the cell in his palm. With deft moves of his thumbs over the tiny keyboard, he searched the pictures, scrutinizing her face in each one. "She's not like that."

Arnold retrieved his phone. "Bullshit." He guffawed. "They never are, are they?" His voice held a good dose of sarcasm.

Trip raised a sharp gaze to his manager. Splotches of color peppered the manager's cheeks. Again, he glanced over his shoulder. Because of the lush greenery, he couldn't even see the pool area.

"Here it is." Arnold's voice called him back.

"What?"

"The stars have aligned. Direct quotes from your announcement of the beach concert. We'd better get our act together. There's a lot to be done. We need to move up the date. Jump on this while it's hot. I'm sure the Del—hell, it's your cousin—Wen…end—"

"Wendee," Trip supplied.

"Of course. Yes, they'll be on board, but better not to be too presumptuous with these things."

When Trip managed to disentangle himself from Arnold, late in the afternoon, by the setting sun, he rushed to Aya's apartment. Dread filled every step. He pulled off his sunglasses to peek through the window, then knocked on her door. An empty, hollow echo replied. Should he be glad? Relieved?

Slowly, he retreated down the stairs. A dark sedan, tinted windows obscuring the view of the passengers, blocked the alleyway. Trip paused mid-step, taking the remaining few slowly. Placing the sunglasses atop of his head, ignoring the macabre feeling this provoked, he peeked through the small window of the shed where she kept her motorcycle. He caught the gleam of the handlebars reflected off the sunset from the other window.

He replaced his glasses, lodged a hand on his hip, scratched his head, and looked around. He and Aya must have crossed paths while he made his way here. Sure he'd see her at the lounge, he cast one last glance at the dark car before wandering down the sidewalk toward the hotel. After confirming her absence at the restaurant, he changed his mind and wandered a circuitous route from the beach to his sister's house.

Still no sign of Aya.

Belaying his nerves, he flexed his fingers. Anxiety flowed like a river. The appearance of twin, dark-colored vehicles in front of the cottage kicked the pace of his pulse. Exact replicas of the vehicle he'd seen in front of the café leading to Aya's small apartment parked along the road made his wrists ache in memory of the handcuffs he'd worn not long ago.

A deep breath whistled through his nose and sighed out his mouth. He reminded himself he'd done nothing wrong. Freedom belonged to him. He firmed his pose and strode to the decorative fence, pausing long enough to flip the latch.

Two stern-faced, suited people perched next to the hood. They stood as he walked by but didn't say a word, not even a nod. Their eyes followed his every movement. Keeping a steady pace, he unlatched the front gate and made his way along the cobbled path to the door. Before he could ascend the stairs, the door flew open, and his mother launched herself at him.

"Thank God, you're okay," she said, smacking his cheek, leaving a waxy feel from her pillowy lips.

Disentangling himself from her embrace, he held her at arm's length. "Why wouldn't I be okay, Stacie?"

A scowl puckered her smooth brow. *Must be due for Botox, then*, he mused. Wrinkles were never allowed. Serpents of sarcasm masked his fear.

She pouted, and tears glistened. "You know I hate it when you call me Stacie."

He rolled his shoulders and cocked his head to the side. He pondered her a moment before speaking. "So it's okay to be our mom now? Didn't you always counsel us that you were too young to be Mom?

137

Wouldn't want any potential suitors to know you had kids, after all."

To her credit, his mother always put him and Evangeline first. True, she attended all their school functions, participated, took them on picnics, vacations...but the twins had to always share her with the latest obsession.

Pent-up resentment like an old leather glove settled over Trip. He glanced over her shoulder, expecting to see some man hovering. Then he gazed into his mother's cornflower blue eyes, taking note of her glossy blonde hair and trim outfit. She did look good. And she did appear concerned, water pooling along the edge of her eyes.

Stacie dropped her manicured hands from his forearms and raised her chin. In that moment, she resembled his formidable grandmother to a T. "That was a long time ago, Travis. I've tried very hard to make it up to you and Evangeline these last years."

He sidestepped her touch. "Yes, by keeping your distance."

"I would have come to the trial." She patted her hair, then folded her hands together at her waist. "But Evangeline reported you didn't want us there."

"So glad you listened," he said and brushed past her to enter the house.

His grandmother stopped him. "You don't have to be cruel."

Shame flushed his body. He removed the sunglasses and lowered his gaze.

Elleah laid gentle fingers on his arm. "People who hurt tend to hurt others. You experienced the same with Kurt."

Shock at her perception made him return her stare. "You fool no one."

Unwilling to give in—emotions tangled with concern over Aya's disappearance, frustrated by his mother's arrival, memories of Kurt, anxiety about the concert—he simply shrugged. Moisture pearled above his lip, but he forced his face into a mask of neutrality, then strode into the kitchen.

Eva rose from one of the chairs, and two more dark-suited people followed her lead.

"Travis," Eva's voice quavered, and he had to tramp down his urge to run. She never used his given name. She was the one who'd nicknamed him "Trip" in the first place from his always stumbling over his too-big feet when they were kids. And it stuck.

Like having run the gambit of evasive maneuvers, avoiding the inevitable bad news, Trip was exhausted. First, his mother, then Gran, and now his sister. What trouble was he in? A tough-as-nails woman of business. When Evangeline Vincent was upset, he had cause to be concerned.

"Travis Vincent." One of the suited men addressed him in a deep baritone. Standing about five eleven, the man had the build of a latent football player with shoulders to match. His meaty fingers held out a cell phone, showing a close-up of Aya's face from that afternoon. "You know this woman?"

Trip squeezed his fingers into fists at his sides to curb the tremble before reaching for the phone. Holding the cell at arm's length, he pondered the picture. "Why?"

"Averyanov Lee Rozanov is a person of interest to our government's safety." His deep-set, dark eyes peered at Trip as though shooting a laser, which could penetrate his brain without his having to confirm one way or another.

"You were photographed together today." The man retrieved his phone, scrolled through the photos, and held up one featuring a smiling Trip next to Aya.

Trip hooked his glasses to the front of his shirt, linked a thumb through his belt loop, and leaned against the door jamb. "So?"

Pulling his suit jacket away from the barrel chest, Mister No Name slipped the phone into a side pocket.

His thinner, scowling partner clicked his tongue. "You are not in a position *not* to be cooperative, Mister Vincent."

In a snap, Trip's anxiety melted away, replaced by an obstinance at being interrogated for some photos taken by his fan base. He crossed a foot over his ankle and forced a smile. What could he and Aya have possibly done? He cocked his head to the side, returning their intense glare. "That right?"

Barrel Chest breathed audibly. "Listen." He held up a hand and glanced at his partner. "We've started on the wrong foot here."

"You think."

The man lowered his chin to his chest, released a small chuckle, and shook his head before straightening again and resuming. "I'm Special Agent John Brown, and this is Bill Williams."

Were the plain names a contrivance to accentuate their nondescript attire, leaving them forgettable to anyone they met? He straightened from the wall, pulled out a chair, and sat down. Placing an elbow on the table, he cupped his chin in his palm. "I'm listening."

Chapter Fifteen

Head lowered to avoid eye contact, she wandered around the beach, sat, and watched a local artist create a multi-tiered sandcastle. How fleeting the construction waiting to be washed away each day on the tide. Unable to contain herself, she strolled to Trip's cottage a mere quarter of a mile away.

Aya leaned against the trunk of a tree and chewed her thumbnail. She couldn't go home. Hell, she had no home. Distraught when fleeing the hotel, she hadn't been quick enough. This inaction compromised the room over the café.

Hot, angry tears of frustration and misery threatened behind her closed lids. To prevent any leak, Aya scrubbed the cuffs of her hands across her eyes. If she gave in now, a river's rush of turbulent sorrow would sweep her away on the rapids.

A shuddered breath shook her, and she bent double to ease the pain. Yes, she should have left this island and Trip. In fact, she could have avoided the affair in its entirety. Yet she didn't. Now, she couldn't go. And…she didn't want to run anymore—didn't want to hide in the shadows of existence.

She angled her body behind the thick foliage, standing opposite Trip's home. From afar, she watched the lovely blonde embrace him before he disappeared inside the house. Then she recognized the stately silhouette of Elleah Fitzgerald just inside the doorway.

Her heart hammered. The two cars out front gave her little doubt about what would be revealed. They'd give Trip and his family the lowdown on her and her subversive ancestors. Described as a dangerous malcontent, a communist threat—despite lack of any evidence—and that would be that. Over. And. Done.

Still, she and Trip were never meant to be, Aya reminded herself. As the granddaughter of one of the most, if not *the most,* notorious presidential assassins in history, she stood little chance of a normal life. Hadn't she learned her lesson a long time ago?

"Fuck." The word hushed, a reflection of bone-dense pain.

She bent her head and cupped her palms across her face. He owned her thoughts. Trip's laughter that afternoon. His head thrown back in passion as he reared, their union leaving him glistening in sweat. The comfort and connection while he held her against him afterward. The way he stroked her hair, his hands lingering on her cheeks before he kissed her. The intensity of his gaze.

Poking her head around the trunk, she scanned the front of the house. Then Aya tilted her face to the darkening sky. A star, a faint pinprick in the distance, showed itself. A gift. The first one. Someone always had to be first. Other stars became visible as the blanket of night shrouded the island.

Aya didn't downplay the significance of the assassination. Considering the blight of that act on Aya's family tree, she could only imagine what Trip had been told about her. Still, that wasn't her, and she owed it to herself to set him straight. Unlike her predecessors, she could do the right thing. She could be the first.

Straightening, she rolled her shoulders in an attempt to release some of the tension. It didn't work. Instead, she tidied her T-shirt, grimaced at her shorts, and adjusted her knapsack. Breathing deeply, she rubbed her hands over the gooseflesh rising on her arms and stepped out from behind the tree to cross the road. Glancing one way then the other, with a careful step, she crossed the road and approached the beach house.

As she drew near, the two officers, who seemed to be attached to the cars, straightened. No question they knew her. Like they'd been expecting her arrival, they flanked her before she could even lay a hand on the gate.

"Radio Williams," the one decorated in a trim moustache said to a stocky ginger above her head. "We have her."

The woman on her right touched a hand to her tie before reaching a finger behind her ear and speaking into a clear receptor. Obviously, a microphone which ran along her jawline. "Agent Williams. Agent Dell and Agent Farmer. We have the suspect."

They hadn't touched her, yet she had no intention of running. They could detain her, but they couldn't hold her. She knew this from experience. They'd already done their worst. They'd revealed who she was and prevented her—again—from having a life she could claim as her own. If she had come clean from the beginning, would that have made any difference? She'd never know. All she wanted was a chance to see Trip one last time. Maybe have an opportunity to explain and try to make him understand.

The ginger-haired woman appraised Aya head to toe. "Pretty dumb of you to come here."

Aya glanced up at Agent Dell. The woman reeked of stale cigarettes. Instead of a comment, Aya shrugged. She had nothing to say. They'd go through their song and dance, and then, contented they'd bullied enough, the feds would let her go.

They stood at the gate, and Aya admired the stone walkway. At one time, somewhere, she'd had a job laying brick and appreciated the artistry. Backbreaking work but satisfying. There was something to be said for hard labor.

The front door opened, and a pool of light spilled across the yard. One then another suited man stepped down. A tremble coursed down her spine.

Then Trip split through the two and barged ahead to stride toward her. Relief flooded her until she caught sight of the glint in his eyes. Hard as rock, his face reflected an unyielding determination. The scars along his cheek stood out white against his tan.

He stopped mere inches from her. She could smell the mixture of sweat and summer breeze clinging to his skin. Her heart ached. She wanted to reach for him. To remind him of their shared moments—the closeness—the connection. Of just that afternoon of joy and carefree delight. But no. His rigid form told her that was all forgotten now.

"You," he said through a panted breath. "You...used...me."

"No," she said and shook her head.

"You lied to me. Everything about you is a lie."

"No."

"Yes," he screamed. "I thought you were different.

I thought you were someone I could be—be with—"

"Stop." The voice carried across on the sea breeze.

They both froze and turned to face the house.

Elleah rushed across the yard. "What is this?" she demanded, standing in front of the assembled people. Even the federal investigators paid attention.

Ginger Hair opened her mouth to speak, but Elleah held up a palm. "I'm not talking to you," she said and flapped her fingers. "Until you arrived, my grandson had finally been happy again."

Trip shrugged his shoulders and flopped his arms against his sides. "She's a stalker, Gran."

"Is she now?" Elleah turned to face Aya. "A stalker?"

Aya turned her head to the side and lowered her chin. She couldn't meet the eyes of a woman who had shown her such kindness at a crucial time in her life.

Elleah's fingers cupped Aya's chin, encouraging her to raise her gaze. "I know you."

Aya nodded.

"Oh my God, my dear." Elleah drew her into a warm embrace. Then her palms cupped Aya's cheeks while she studied her face.

"Wh-what is this?" Trip stepped forward and pulled his grandmother away, placing himself between the two women. "Shit. I don't care."

Then he dropped his arms to his sides, and tears trickled down her cheeks.

"I saw you at the courthouse. I thought you believed in me. I'm so stupid." He shook his head, glancing up to the stars. "But what are you?" He returned his gaze to her. He breathed heavily. Moisture glistened on his lashes. "What are you?" he repeated.

"Some stalker. Someone looking to make a name for herself, living up to your family's legacy."

"No," Aya said, but the sound erupted in a coarse whisper. "No, you have to listen to me. I knew there was more to the story. Your grandmother—"

"Leave her out of this."

"No." Aya's tone firmed. She squared her shoulders and raised her chin. "She had shown me a great kindness at the lowest time of my life, and I owed it to her to return—"

"Return what?" He dragged his hand down his face. The crisp hair crunched like sandpaper. Eyes hard like shards of broken glass, he leaned toward her. "Just another angle. I should have known from the very first night. Some fancy fuck." He sneered the words. "You bagged the pop star...is that it?"

"Enough." Elleah raised her voice and placed a hand on his shoulder to force him around.

Trip shrugged the older woman's grip off. "I don't care," he said, facing Aya again, almost nose to nose. "I don't care."

Aya lifted her palms, opened her mouth to speak, but the lump in her throat prevented words. Her chin wobbled, and she bit her lip to control the movement.

"I fuck chicks like you all the time. You were nothing special."

Elleah turned Trip and slapped his face—hard. Even the agents straightened, and an audible rush of breath cascaded the action.

Had Aya been punched in the gut? She wanted nothing more than to crouch over the wound. So barren of feeling, his harsh words penetrated to her core, leaving her hollow. She forced herself to stand tall.

"No. If only you'd—" She coughed and repeated, adding strength she didn't feel behind the sound. "If you'd only listen…"

But he had turned from her and stalked away, each footfall sounding like a blow which Aya endured.

Chapter Sixteen

Past his grandmother, ignoring the sting on the side of his face, Trip marched back to the house.

His mother caught his arm on the bottom step, a hand on his wrist.

"Don't...touch...me," he said between gritted teeth, shaking her hand loose. "Don't come near me."

He snubbed his sister, took the stairs to the loft above the garage two at a time, slammed the door, and went directly to the liquor cabinet. After locating the tall bottle of vodka, he cradled it for a moment in his palm before twisting the cap. The aroma drifted to tantalize his urge.

Moving to the garden window, Trip leaned against the casing and pondered the night sky. Then he nodded, slapped a hand on his thigh, strode across the room, and reached for a glass from the kitchenette. His fingers trembled. Turmoil coiled in his stomach. He weighed the bottle in his left hand to the weight of the heavy glass tumbler in his right.

"Fuck." With relish, he threw the goblet across the room where it smashed into the rock face of the fireplace. The shards haloed the hearth. He slumped down on the corner of the bed, dangling the bottle between his knees. Then he tilted the bottle and guzzled the contents directly. The burn slid down his throat and into his empty stomach. Trip swiped at the moisture in his eyes and upended the liquor again.

Better than anything the doctor could prescribe. He craved oblivion and fast. Emotions swirled, and his thoughts were disruptive. Kurt—Aya—his grandmother—sister—mother. He needed to stop thinking.

He laid a palm against his cheek.

How could he have possibly thought Aya was different from any of the other women he'd bedded? Hadn't he known better? Hell, you'd think he'd have had a clue when she seduced him after just meeting him at the lounge. She'd been clever to evoke his interest by not actively pursuing him afterward. More ingenious than most, for sure. As the agents had said, she always did her homework.

But what was her connection to his family? The rubbish about her repaying a debt.

"Who cares?" He drank deeply.

Trip prowled the circumference of the room. "No, no, not Aya." Trip shook his head, a hand behind his neck. "Averyanov Lee Rozanov." The name burned hot on his tongue. He gasped for air and wiped the sweat from his temples. When would he learn? Everyone betrayed him. Everyone.

Never show the soft underbelly, he reminded himself. People couldn't resist grabbing the knife to stab.

A soft knock sounded.

"Go away."

"No," his sister shouted back and pounded the wooden door.

The obstinacy of her ignoring his command reminded him he was wrong. Not everyone betrayed him. Evangeline had always been loyal. Family aside.

He banged his foot on the floorboards. "Fuck off."

Of course, he'd never include his twin in his description of "everyone." She'd always be a stand-alone. The fighter in the family. The strong one. Someone they all leaned on. A carbon copy of their grandmother.

"Shit. Fuck—whatever." He banged the cuff of his hand against his forehead. He slid off the side of the bed. On his knees, he rocked back and forth. He didn't know what he was doing anymore.

He looked at the bottle and then across the room to the dresser mirror, hating the reflection. "What a sorry state." Really, what had he amounted to? Tired eyes stared out of a pale, blotched face. Unkempt hair stuck out at all angles, and he resembled a bum better suited to living out of a dumpster than in the opulent house—the home his sister provided. The generation dwelling purchased to bring family together.

He couldn't face them—his family—or Eva—no one. He couldn't face himself. He hung his head and squeezed his eyes shut to block the image of his own face. Clarity showed him he had failed at everything—failed Kurt, Arnold, everyone.

The banging of the door echoed throughout the room. "Let me in," Eva insisted. The door knob rattled, reminding him of when they were kids and she'd stubbornly hound him until he gave in to her.

He gulped at the contents of the bottle. Burped and held the container up to the light. A third gone and barely a buzz. "Not this time."

"Every time—"

"No," he said, glancing toward the entry, ensuring

she hadn't managed to open it.

"Yes," she returned.

He took another swig and stood, swayed a bit, grinned, and then shook his head like a bull. "Fuck off."

"No. You fuck off."

Trip staggered to the large wooden door and laughed despite himself. Breathing heavily, he laid his forehead against the carved oak. A welcomed dizziness had started to fog his brain. "This isn't funny." He thumped his head once, then twice and again. Stars shimmered in his vision, and he rested his forehead on the cool surface. Hot liquid streamed into his eyes.

He reached fingers to wipe it away. The iron scent overpowered the liquor. He'd split his brow. For spite, he hammered his head harder. His brain felt rattled.

"Stop that," she yelled. "I'm not laughing."

"It is kinda funny, though," Trip said after a long pause.

"Listen, whoever you think you're bashing your brains in for just isn't worth it," she said, voice gentle. "But you are."

"Worth falling for a stalker."

"Falling…"

A long silence followed. Was she still there? He laid his ear against the polished wood now blemished with blood. He could almost hear her heart beating in unison with his. Eva wouldn't leave him. He'd let her in eventually, yet shame kept him from opening the door. How many times must she pick him up after he had tumbled? Wasn't he supposed to be the big brother?

He felt rather than heard a thump on the door. He imagined her forehead just on the other side, as though the door were glass instead of wood. They mirrored each other.

"You sure?"

After so long a silence, her voice startled him, and he stepped back.

"Sure?" he asked. "Of what?" He'd forgotten the thread of conversation.

Eva chuckled, and Trip narrowed his eyes, trying to see through the oak. She was laughing.

"I'm not laughing at you," she said, reading his mind like she usually did.

"What then?"

"I'm asking…sure you've fallen for her? Sure she's a stalker? What are you sure of?" she asked and shook the door handle. "Enough. Let me in."

"Huh." The sound erupted from his larynx. "Sure of nothin'."

"What's the problem, then? With the parade of women through this house, I'd have thought this would be just part of the deal."

Trip shook his head. "You heard the agents. Fucking granddaughter of a murderer. An assassin, for Christ's sake. Hard-core, cold-blooded—calculating."

"Gran doesn't think so," she countered. "Anyway, so what?"

"So what?" Trip straightened from the door, swayed, and braced a hand along the molding to steady, swiping the blood to clear his vision. "What do you mean, so what? She knew me. She tracked me down. She's as cold-blooded as her grandsire. Maybe even more so *is* so what."

"You deaf, too?" she said, an edge to her tone. "Everyone who listens to music knows you. Who cares who her grandfather was? We've no great ancestry, or had you forgotten about great-granddad Declan who locked his own—and only—daughter in an asylum for having an affair with a married man?"

Trip barked out a laugh. "That's a little different than killing the president."

"*She* didn't kill the president. Hell, not only wasn't she born then, how can she be responsible for something her grandfather did? Get your head out of your ass."

"You get *your* head out of your ass. She's on the government watchlist. That's something. She knew all about me. Attended the trial." Trip banged his palm flat on the door. Then he lifted the bottle to his lips, missed, and spilled the liquid down his shirt. "Go away. I don't want you here."

"Too bad. My house. Remember?"

"Only 'cause I agreed," he said, his words starting to slur. He concentrated his focus on the mouth of the bottle to hit the target and tilted it again. This time, he met his aim. Fiery liquid coated his tongue and throat. How much more until oblivion? Passing out shouldn't be far off now. Then he could forget about those deep eyes burrowing into his very soul, demanding him to expect more—of himself.

"Still my house. Stop being an asshole and let me in."

Her words broke his train of thought. He hung his head, chin to chest, shoulders rounded. "I—I don't like the way you're talking to me."

"I'd be nicer if you let me in."

"No, you won't." He shook his head and dropped the bottle to the floor. It landed with a thud on the carpet but didn't break.

"I will...promise."

Her voice coaxed him, reminding him of their history and that she remained the one person he could always trust. Eva never broke her promises.

He stepped back and unlocked the door.

Chapter Seventeen

Aya's hands shook. She flexed her fingers and pulled the cell from her pocket. Holding the phone close to her thigh, she activated the screen and typed a quick text to the only person in the world she trusted.

Help me.

Then the agents confiscated the appliance.

As a lawyer, manager, and long-time confidant, Maury would do whatever he could—if anything.

They ushered her to the back seat and sandwiched her between the ginger and one of the agents who'd exited the house with Trip. A bulky man, he had a face that looked as though it had been used for boxing practice, complete with a cauliflower ear and a nose as an add-on feature.

Shifting, she shrugged, folded her arms across her chest, and slouched down in the seat to get as comfortable as possible given the situation. Of course, relaxation was impossible. The object being to piss the authorities off.

Ginger agent rolled her eyes and turned to stare out the window.

Past experience and logic told her she couldn't be held in custody for long. They had nothing—not really. Always suspicions. No evidence. Besides, she worked, filed her taxes annually, albeit from a P.O. box from her home state. Still, they got their fair share. What did they have to complain about?

Except, she and her family featured prominently on the watchlist. However, this was the first time she'd been picked up by a party of four. She guessed someone like Trip warranted celebrity treatment.

She didn't allow complacency. Experience warned these federal agents, bored from chasing useless people like herself, could be as miserable as they wanted. Prolong her suffering, waylay, insist, and create something from nothing. They could crave action and disrupt until they provoked a reaction. She'd have to keep her wits. In reality, if these agents wanted, she hadn't a leg to stand on, as the saying went.

With little to no verbal interaction, they crossed the Coronado Bridge. The driver zig-zagged through San Diego, and she quickly lost track of her surroundings. One turn eclipsed into another, and she wasn't even sure they remained in San Diego, though she assumed they must. She didn't think they'd take her all the way into LA. But really, what did she know at this point?

As they turned north on the highway, seeming to leave San Diego behind, on I-5, Aya remembered the closest office stood just off the Sorrento Parkway, closer to La Jolla. Ever since her first encounter with federal agents, she had made it a point to know all their main locations.

She twisted her fingers together in her lap. "So stupid," she mumbled and shook her head.

"What's that?" Ginger turned her attention to Aya.

Aya ignored her. True, she'd been stupid. How many times had she told herself to never get involved? Never take a relationship farther than a single night. Hell, never engage in a relationship. In order to be free of this family stain, she must sacrifice the need for…what? Nothing she could ever do would release her from the past.

The answer was so simple she nodded and chuckled. "Everything."

"What?" The tall agent in the front seat pivoted back to stare at her. His brow creased, eyes narrowed, and his ears seemed to create a hovering effect for his head they were so large.

Aya turned her head and glowered out the window. A muted reflection stared through the backdrop of passing highway lights. She longed to cry—to lie down, curl up, and engage in a deep, heart-wrenching cry. The feel-sorry-for-herself, the-world-was-coming-to-an-end big, bad bawl.

Then she giggled, the sound slightly unhinged, at the notion. This caused three heads except the driver to swivel in her direction. She didn't bother to acknowledge. Whenever she found herself in the back of a car of this make and model meant her life as she knew it, for that moment in time, had come to a crashing end.

She'd started over so many times from the ashes she claimed as her life. Aya would be amazed if she even had tears left to shed. In the past, tears for her were more akin to an average person going to the bank and expecting a fortune to have amassed where they hadn't invested anything. But now, everything had changed. Trip made life different.

She loved him.

Yet as irony would have it, she had the fortune in several banks distributed throughout the states and elsewhere. Protected as only Maury could do. She simply lacked the ability to find someone to share her prosperity—to enjoy mutual professional successes. Her throat clogged, and no surprise, she had more than enough tears left to shed. She fought to hold them back. She needed to remain calm and strong to get through this. Then she would start *again*.

Aya coughed and cursed inwardly. Anger flushed across her skin, leaving a ripple of gooseflesh in its wake.

Her computer would surely be busted. All her work. At any given time, Aya would have material for ten to twenty potential musical artists as leads for her songs. Maury did the same, but their data did not mirror the other's—more like collaboration when she had a new songbook ready. She kept a database of music. The artist or band who wrote the songs, the vocals, chart toppers, what worked, and the awards. Then she would match existing or in progress non-published music to the artists, and she would leave it Maury to broker a deal.

She remembered broaching to Maury the opportunity of selling her music to *Iron Clad*, Trip's band. He hadn't been keen, but then there'd been his last cover. The photo taken at the graveyard and Trip's vacant gaze, his smile a mask. Aya perceived such sadness—an echo of her own longing.

Craziness. Yet she remembered the youth in his grandmother's kitchen, and her heart ached. At that moment, she'd sealed her fate and made the decision. Now, she sat like a casserole ready for the oven.

What choice had she had? He'd reeled her to him, like a worm on a hook. Shortly after the album, the gossip, failed rehab, the accident, then the trial, and all the media attention.

Like a witch hunt, the masses made their opinions known in the court of public disgrace. Social feeds broadcasted everything from substance abuse to liaisons, all but killing any reputation Trip and *Iron Clad* may have held onto. The process proved an echo of the many times she'd been thronged by reporters, wanting to know what it was to be the granddaughter of a presidential assassin. The ordeal for Trip being all too familiar, Aya couldn't stop herself from attending the trial to see for herself.

And he saw her, too. No doubt when their eyes connected across the foyer, she knew as sure as her next breath, she had to see him again. Regardless of the risks.

Drawn by the romance, the musical legacy of him and his family, and the kindness of his grandmother, Aya repeatedly pushed all thoughts of the inevitable consequences aside. Like a swimmer who misjudged the ocean current, she'd been swept away and unable to get back to shore.

Other than being a passing fancy, Aya retained no illusion that Trip would lose any sleep over her. She'd be just another notch—one who might be remembered due to being wanted by the feds. A little notoriety.

"Ha," she barked, and then covered her mouth as though coughing.

All for a song. But…he had sung it. She rolled her shoulders and tried to access her bravery for the next phase of this stupid dance with her escorts.

Instead, she lowered her head and hummed the bars of a new song written for him. Though, it seemed to fit her just as well. Soon, the lyrics followed:

"I fell hard into addiction's arms,
I had it all, I had a life,
Then I let it go, I didn't bother to fight,
Not a word, I was bathed in the light."

Tears swam, blurring her vision, while the agent turned in his seat to watch. Lips pursed, he didn't say a word.

Unconcerned any longer in pretense, she blinked until they splashed onto her cheeks. Unable to stop the flow of music, Aya continued.

"Then there's you, and I let you go,
You melted away, like the spring-thawed snow,
Not until I woke from addiction's embrace,
Did I realize I should have gave chase.
Never should I have let you go,
I don't know where I'm supposed to go,
But I want you back, oh, can't you see,
Addiction's gone, he's finally left me."

The last line emerged a croak, and she pressed her lips together. Aya swiped the moisture off her cheeks, sniffed, then lowered her hands to her lap. With finality, she laced her fingers together.

The car turned off the main highway, and ahead she saw the squat gray building. Their final destination. She just needed to get through it, whatever "it" proved to be this time—be on her way and start again.

Again.

Chapter Eighteen

Exhaustion competed with hyper-energy. His leg vibrated while he digested the events of the last twenty-four hours. Highs to lows, Eva spared little sympathy while he sobered up. She'd made him feel a goddamned fool. And he was.

The dawn had barely broken, and Trip stood with his palm flat against the brick façade surrounding the cold fireplace, pondering his next steps. Two urchin shells, one larger than the other, sat so the larger, faded purple fossil looked like the parent to the smaller, which leaned on a diagonal against its base. Trip smiled and gently placed the smaller of the two on top so they more resembled a spiky snowman. Moving these ornaments from one aspect to the other had been an ongoing, unspoken game he and his sister participated in since they were children. He preferred the snowman. Within a few days, she'd see the change and readjust until he noticed, and on the game would go.

Moving relics didn't help. He shook his head and turned his back to the fireplace. He paced to the bay window and replayed the exchange.

"How could you stand by and not defend her?" Her arms flung into the air in exasperation. "You didn't even question. Simply accepted what they, strangers, I might add, said—idiot."

Trip tried to speak, but his words muddled, unable

to overcome the thickness of his tongue.

"You should know better than most"—Eva poked his chest with her forefinger, her cheeks flushed and stare fiery—"what it's like to be prosecuted through innuendo."

Trip's mouth had lost all moisture. He couldn't speak if he wanted to.

She breathed hard, her chest heaving. "Christ, do you have any idea how many people are on our country's 'watchlist?' " She made air quotes with her fingers. "What a joke. The color of your skin, country of origin, or your ancestry can get you on that database."

By three in the morning, he made ready to break Aya free of whatever cell they were holding her in. He had to hear her side. He stood from the edge of the bed where he'd been perched for the last hour.

Eva shook her head and pushed him back down. "Just like you, brother. Going off half-cocked, no clue as to where you're going, how you'll get there, or what you'll do once you arrive."

Fed up, Trip flared, standing again, arms flung wide. "Okay, smartass. What's your idea, then?"

She clicked her tongue and tapped a nail against her teeth, pacing back and forth. "Wait until the morning, and I'll make a couple of calls. I'm bound to know someone who knows someone."

As a professional concierge, Eva's job depended on six degrees of separation to get what her clients wanted. Trip didn't doubt his sister's ability. Still, his heart raced, and his stomach folded in on itself. "Leave her there all night?" Trip made for the door. "No way."

Eva caught him by the wrist. "Time enough in the

morning to be a hero," she said, her tone gentle. "Let me help."

Three hours later, he could wait no more. Using the time zones to her advantage, Eva had been working the phones while he prowled the premises. She'd had some success, and a lawyer was dropping by.

Trip strode into her study. "Not good enough," he said. "I have to do something."

Eva followed him back into the hall where he collected his jacket when the doorbell rang.

Now, an immaculate man in a dark, three-piece, tailored suit sat across from Trip at his sister's kitchen table. His presence filled the room easily. The wide-set eyes, which didn't shift or sway in conversation, gave the impression he knew what he needed to know, regardless of what you might say to the contrary.

Unsettled, Trip pushed his sleeves up over his elbows and glanced at his sister. His fingers strummed the tabletop.

Eva stood side on, behind the kitchen counter, seemingly absorbed in the last of the coffee dripping into the pot. In the heavy silence, the drop could be heard across the room. Dark circles rimmed her eyes, accentuating the pale and drawn features.

He'd done this, Trip thought. What a mess. When was the last time he'd expressed any curiosity about her life or the business she gave so much of herself to? Did she even have someone special? He wrinkled his brow and rubbed his temples. He didn't think so. Normally, she would hold any visitor in rapt conversation, leaving Trip to brood. But not today, it seemed.

This fellow's arrival seemed too coincidental to Eva's phone inquiries and Aya's predicament.

The broad-shouldered man lifted a hand to adjust the slender, rust-colored tie. The wide brow and firm jawline gave every impression of a "man's man." Someone who, despite the prissy dress, anyone would want to have a beer and share a good story with.

"I was on my way to see Aya when I received your call." The man spoke to Eva. "I hope you don't mind my coming. I know you invited me, still…"

Eva turned to address Trip. "I thought you'd want to meet the man Aya called."

Trip accepted a mug of coffee from her and nodded, all attention focused. Ironically, despite Trip's own discomposure, this man represented the type of guy Trip wished Arnold could have been. Even though he hadn't done anything as yet, instinctively, Trip knew this to be the kind of fellow to get a deal done.

Hell, truth be told, this was a man Trip wanted to be. Jealousy flared hot across his skin, leaving pinpricks of anxiety in its wake. Here was the hero of the story. Someone dependable to be there when called—no matter the time or location.

Eva handed a steaming cup of tea to the stranger who introduced himself as Maury Chapman, Aya Rose's legal representative and agent. She'd apparently sent him a text when the federal agents picked her up yesterday, and he'd come straight away from Canada.

Trip lowered his gaze. Where this Maury didn't hesitate, Trip had reacted in anger and resentment, only thinking of himself. He drained the contents of the coffee and stared at the grounds left at the bottom of the cup. That's what he felt like, the leftover dregs. Something to be washed down the drain.

Maury hovered an aristocratic nose over the rim,

breathing in the fragrant steam. "Thank you," he said with an incline of his head toward Trip's sister. "My favorite. English Breakfast. Lovely."

Eva brought the coffee carafe to the table, and Trip refilled his mug, leaving the sediment to accumulate with the new. He pondered Maury a moment. Agent? Lawyer? "What would a waitress need with an agent?"

Maury laughed. "Surely, you know by this point, there's significantly more to our young friend—"

"Yes," Trip huffed.

"She's the author of *Iron Clad's* gold records."

Trip half-rose from his seat, which tipped then fell over. "What?" Turning, he straightened the chair and sat back down, hands braced along the table's edge.

"You've been playing her songbook," Maury said, his mouth quirked, deepening the lines etching the contours. "Doing a great job, by the way. Congratulations."

The information rocked Trip. He opened then closed his mouth. How could this be? Surely, he'd know? He needed time to absorb this revelation. He sniffed the aromatic coffee before taking a sip. The heat scalded his tongue. He wished at this moment his sister had had the good sense to spike the liquid with something a little more powerful than caffeine and creamer. He stared across at the man who smiled blandly, seeming to enjoy his beverage in small sips.

Trip ran fingers through his hair and dragged the hand down his face. "I don't understand... Wilkes Booth...the name on the songbook...I knew was an alias, but I thought—"

"You thought the author a man," Maury supplied and chuckled. Vivid gray eyebrows, matching the goatee and moustache, provided a complement to his dark features. The man had skin the color of sun-soaked cedar. The wavy white hair left Trip wondering if it were dyed to be so uniform—no salt and pepper for this guy. "Everyone does."

Trip wanted to hate him. Maury presented a further reminder of his many failings. In that moment, Trip wanted to be the person Aya turned to. Given the chance, he could be *that* man. All he wanted to do was fix the wrongs. His foot tapped the tiles, heel thumping. He couldn't bring Kurt back, but he could be there for the woman he loved.

"Why are you here?" Trip blurted and set his cup down with a bang. The liquid sloshed over the side.

Eva's gaze flew to his, and she sucked in her breath.

Maury's sharp brown eyes widened slightly, the yellow flecks piercing.

Now, with clarity of focus, Trip realized Maury, too, held his emotions under tight control.

Maury inclined a chin toward Eva. "Your sister called me."

Eva coughed to clear her throat. "You flew in this morning?" she asked, taking her own seat, mug in hand, and folded a leg under her backside as she did so.

Maury pushed his chair back slightly, crossed his legs, and leaned an elbow on the table. "Yes," he said with an accent Trip couldn't place. "I made the arrangements right away. Unfortunately, with connections and delays from Toronto…" He let the words peter off and shrugged his shoulders.

Why couldn't Trip have acted as quickly? Perhaps had he responded with any kindness, Aya wouldn't have been harassed in the first place. He directed his anguish at the stranger. "Shouldn't you have gone straight to where they're holding her?" An edge colored his tone. He wiped moist palms on his thighs.

Maury's eyes crinkled, but the flash of the gaze remained. With a fluid motion, he lifted the tea cup to take another sip and nodded to Eva. "This hits the spot." He sighed, then returned his focus to Trip. "Though I came for Aya, I realized about halfway here my coming was a mistake."

What little self-control Trip may have had fled. His arms flew wide. "How? She needs you. Jesus, she called you for help." Trip wrapped suddenly chilled fingers around the mug. It clattered a bit, and he released his grip, folding them instead. "Surely you don't mean to leave her there?"

Eva's gentle gaze found his, then she smiled in that all-knowing way a sister does when she'd been proven right. Color dotted her cheeks.

Yes, damn it. He cared more than he admitted. Certainly, this was not the time to profess his love for a woman he'd let go. Especially not now when he'd been proven the heel and across from him sat the real hero.

Trip sighed and lowered his head. How could he have stormed off and allowed Aya to be taken away without even letting her have a say? Without listening. As Eva pointed out, he knew better than most that there was always more to the story.

He had to go to Aya. *Now.* Emotions swamped him, forcing him to take a breath and stare out the window above the sink. He flattened his palms against the table. The tremors coursed through him like icy shards, and he crossed his ankles to steady the shake.

Think. He couldn't think. He pictured Aya, small and daunted by the four federal agents. Imagining her in a cell, alone…or worse, surrounded by other criminals…

"I mean…" Trip floundered and pulled his sleeves back down over his forearms, returning his gaze to Maury.

Even from what little time they'd spent together, he knew Aya was tough. From the beginning, she'd offered no nonsense. Straightforward and relentlessness formed part of her aura and allure. That strength attracted Trip as much as her compassion. Everything she offered, he needed—in spades. A confidence he wished he could harness. Her seeming ability to see through him and understand what made him tick like no one else—not even his sister. Yet she didn't care what she saw, because she cared about him. Inherently, he knew that and still had walked away without helping—even offering to help.

"You know," Maury broke the silence, interrupted the turmoil. "Conviction is only a platitude unless challenged with actual choice."

Trip started. "What's that supposed to mean?"

"We can all sit on the sidelines and wax poetically, spouting all kinds of opinions." He lifted one leg a fraction of an inch and tugged on his pant leg to straighten an already perfect pleat. He resettled his leg. "But until we are faced with having to stand by those principles, despite what may be popular with the crowd…well…then they are just words, aren't they?"

Shame licked Trip's cheeks, and perspiration pearled above his lip.

Maury slapped his hands together and stood. "But

I'm not telling you anything you don't already know."

Trip rose, too. "But you haven't said why you're not going to her. She's not done anything...has she?" he asked, his voice spiked at the end.

"Alas, she really doesn't want or need me." Maury reached to retrieve his overcoat. His gaze traced Trip head to toe. "You're not what I expected," he said in a voice deep like a narrator of a great story. Every syllable packed with significance.

Agitation flooded Trip's bloodstream, causing a flush to mount. He brushed a hand across his hair. His head ached, and his stomach rolled. He was coming apart at the seams. "Good to know."

He grabbed his mug, thought better of it, and instead pushed his hands into his pockets. With effort he maintained a straight face. "You didn't answer me, though. What kind of agent, ah, lawyer, are you anyway that you would come here and not go directly to your client?"

Maury stared at him, gaze stony, his coat hung lightly over his arm like it belonged there. "Aya likely regretted contacting me the moment she sent the text message. And I, like a fool, reacted right away. I have worried over her like a distant father for years now. Truth is...I came for me. Then when your sister made inquiries, and our mutual friend called...well...I know of you, of course, and the connection. So I came here. Curiosity, I guess."

The man glanced down at Eva. His smile widened. Dimples appeared amongst the lines. He rubbed his palms together. "I can't tell you how often I had hoped she'd ask me to help. But she is so proud and determined. She'd never want me to fuss. Though I am her musical agent, she keeps our roles very clear. Aya writes from wherever she is whenever the mood sweeps her, which fortunately for me is often. Then she sends the compositions to me to sell. She likes to maintain strict lines."

"Sounds like her," Trip admitted.

"Yes," Maury agreed. "And then, like a wish being granted, she did ask for my help. I had to come."

"You're very confusing," Eva said, shaking her head.

Maury cocked his head to the side. "She needs someone to look out for her and someone to be with her. I'm going to be what she wants—someone to look out for her. You"—he pointed at Trip—"are the one she wants."

Trip felt the weight of his words and the truth. He stood, the table separating the two men.

"Well, I must be off." Maury turned to go.

"But—"

"Yes?" Maury scanned his face.

Trip found his voice. "What about Aya? What will happen to her?"

The business-like façade seemed to fade away, and Maury stood like a father before a suitor who fell woefully short of the measure.

Trip gulped his shame. In front of this man, he felt no better than a child who had been caught with his hand in the cookie jar. "She's been hauled off into custody. She needs a lawyer...a friend."

Maury nodded. "Oh, I'll do my part—have already. She's being released..." He checked his wristwatch. "Likely now. But I'll not embarrass her further by going to her. As I'm sure you've guessed, it's not the first time. I always wish it would be the last, that they'd leave her be, but...well, I don't think that will be the case until she trusts in someone enough to settle down." He scanned the room in general, raised his chin to Eva, and turned. "Someday, perhaps."

"What does that mean?" Trip asked.

Maury paused at the door. "Aya is tough. She'll get through this and be on her way. I only wish the best for her. Someone to love her for who she is, not what an ancient relative from a long-ago time did... Alas, I say too much."

He gave Trip one last look and nodded to Eva. "Thank you for your hospitality."

Chapter Nineteen

The sun glared, almost blinding, as Aya stepped out of the large gray structure. Like most operational-type government buildings, the nondescript front entrance had been ugly and bland, but air conditioned compared to the concrete landing outside. How dare the sky be so blue and endless, the ocean so inviting, when she craved clouds and gloom to match the sadness threatening to overwhelm her heart? She knew better than to let herself believe—even for a moment—that she could have a life of her own and a love of her own. Add that Trip was a famous personality. "Ha." No, she chided herself, she couldn't pick someone plain and ordinary. She fell for the most controversial artist she could find.

She tilted her head and scowled into the heavens. The dazzle of the light drew the tears she had managed to hold at bay during the interrogation. She let them flow. Just for a moment. The drops dripped from her chin. She'd allow herself this small release before she stored this love, along with so many other forbidden emotions, back away into her secret vault of heartache. Then she would move on. Always moving on.

She leveled her gaze and squinted, swiping the last of the tears away, and blew her nose. She pulled her sunglasses from her bag and positioned them over her ears, then drew a deep breath and considered her options.

Though her inventory of possessions remained small and portable, everything was located at her apartment above the café. "Shit."

In all likelihood, most of what she owned had been tossed and broken at this point from the feds rummaging through her stuff. For sure, her computer would be missing, or at least, the hard drive itself. Had she backed up her latest work? She bit her lip and considered. She fist-punched the air. Yes.

"Thank God."

No real loss if she had to replace the machine or the drive. So long as they hadn't damaged her guitar. What about her bike? She'd soon find out.

She meandered down the steps. Stupid to have contacted Maury. At least, he was smart enough to just see to her release and not embarrass her by coming in person. Her humiliation compounded, and she shook her head. Would it ever stop? Could she not be left alone?

"They keep searching for something they will never find," she muttered aloud, hitching her fingers in her top jeans pocket, twisting to stare up at the building. After all these years, would they, whomever "they" were who'd put her on a watchlist, never realize Aya held no interest in assassinating anyone? Certainly, she couldn't change what had happened in the past, even if no one would ever let her forget it.

Turning to face the road, she looked one way then the other. Traffic droned by. People going here and there. Highway noise filled the air. Situation normal, as though her life hadn't shattered in the last twenty-four hours. She reached the sidewalk and considered her next move, drawing her hand free to swipe her hair back from her brow. The sweat gathered in her hairline.

One foot followed the other, and she trudged up the road on auto pilot. "Where to now?"

"Home."

The deep, velvet tones caused her step to falter, as though there were a crack in the concrete. Her head whipped round until her eyes found his. "Wha-what are you doing here?"

He sat astride her Indian motorcycle, cradling the helmet in his lap. "I'm here for you."

Though he looked every inch the boyfriend she longed for, in that moment she recalled his words, spat so icy and cold. Her thoughts spun, making her dizzy. What was he doing here? How did he even know where to find her? After all they had shared, why hadn't he given her a chance to explain?

Her fingers flexed then fisted. She wanted to lean on something—someone for support, but there was nothing—no one. Always alone. Forever on her own.

"Puh," she breathed, striving to stand tall. "Here for me. What a load of crap."

He shook his head and lowered his chin. His long face and strong jaw appeared ashen. Smudges shadowed his eyes. He looked hungover. Likely was. That would make sense.

Swiping fingers under the lenses of her glasses and across her eyes, she ensured no moisture remained. "How can you be here for me?" She planted her feet, willing herself not to go to him, unsure. "You know what—who I am. Or don't you remember? Some stalker, right? I'm just someone who fancied a *fuck* with a celebrity, waiting to get my name in the papers. Be famous myself. Did you lose your memory in the bottle again?"

Spoken harshly, the words seared her tongue. He winced as though she had struck him, and his head dipped farther between his shoulders, chin almost to his chest. He raised a hand and ran it down his cheek. She imagined she could hear the scratch of stubble along his palm. Wounded, hooded eyes glanced up to peer across at her.

But Aya was unmoved. She wanted to hurt him. She wanted him to feel the pain of loss like she did. Feel the humiliation.

She gazed around, curbing the urge to run and flee the scene. Get away from him and the feelings he provoked. She had to move on without him, get her head out of the fantasy of being with him. The sooner the better.

She started to walk away, then remembered her motorcycle.

Retracing her steps, she stomped back, hand on her hip, glad of the glasses that hid most of her own blotched features with their over-sized dark lenses. "Get off my bike."

Obligingly, he got up and stepped to the side. He waited for her to straddle the seat and then handed her the black helmet.

She slammed the helmet on her head, stood the motorcycle erect, and reached her right leg to kick off the stand. Her hands caressed the handlebars, and she hesitated to ignite the engine. Her thumb hovered over the button. Tears stung her eyes, and her throat clogged. Why had he come here? He could have just let her be on her way. She brushed her chin on her shoulder and gripped the rubber tighter. Her knuckles whitened. She coughed and squeezed her eyes tightly closed.

A hand grasped her forearm. "Aya."

She shook her head. "Don't you mean Averyanov Lee Rozanov? Granddaughter of Lee—"

"No." The single word shot into the air halted all other noise around them. His hands rose to her shoulders, turning her toward him. He gently removed her glasses. "I mean Aya Rose."

Aya forced her eyes open and looked at him. His face seemed set, determined, and at that moment she didn't know what she expected. The flecks of gray in his ocean green eyes seared through to her soul, holding her in place. Hair damp with sweat curled around his ears. His foot shot out and kicked the stand in place. He eased her up from the seat and held her at arm's length.

"Aya Rose..." His breath shuddered. "I've been a complete fuck-up."

She started to shake her head and protest, but he shushed her with a finger across her lips.

He tenderly pulled the helmet off and dropped it to the grass. His lips pursed, and his brow wrinkled. He shook his head. "You've woken me from nightmares of my own creation. In my bleakest moment, you were there, and you gave me strength whether you meant to or not."

"No, I..."

He nodded. "You did. I didn't want to see what was right in front of me." His thumb brushed her jaw, and his fingers curled behind her neck. "I didn't think I needed—no, strike that. I didn't want to need anyone again. Kurt was like a brother to me. A best friend and soul mate..." His words trailed, but his gaze stayed locked and focused on her. "Until he wasn't. I felt betrayed. Angry, really. Hateful and inept and took it out on everyone around me. I didn't *want* to feel anymore. I didn't *want* to *want* you. But I did."

She coughed, and her fist rose to her mouth. "I'm not a stalker," she managed at last, the words sounding strangled. "Your grandmother had been kind to me once—"

"She told me."

"She did?"

He nodded.

"When I heard what happened, I had to come."

He smiled, and his features lightened, a weight released off his chest, and color rose in his cheeks. He stared for a long moment, seeming to consider her, then cocked his head to the side, nodding. He eyes crinkled, and a mischievous light swam in the current of his gaze. "Still, you are kinda like a stalker."

Aya stiffened, stood tall, and squared her shoulders, wishing she were taller. "I am not."

The lines around his lips deepened, and a dimple appeared as his smile spread wide. "Yeah, you are."

She bunched her hands into fists at her side. "This isn't funny."

Trip glanced over his shoulder, toward the imposing gray government building, and then back at her and nodded. "Come on. It is."

"Are you serious?" She started to step away, but he held onto her, his fingers tightening.

Had he lost his senses? Was he drunk? He didn't smell of booze. "You can't be serious," she repeated.

"Think of the songs we'll write together."

"Songs?" The word launched as a croak. "Wait.

What?"

He nodded, and his eyes danced. "That's right. You know all about me. Now I know all about you."

Aya lowered her gaze and stared at the ground. Ants moved in a frenzy at the base of a tree, and her pulse raced while she considered his words. Finally, light dawned. "Maury."

"That's right," Trip confirmed. "Nice fellow, if you can get by his being a teetotaler."

"Tea?" Aya felt mystified. Dizzy spots invaded her vision. Had she just stepped off the edge of the world? What had happened? Maury was here. She glanced around, up and down the street, but no one stood out. She couldn't understand what was happening.

"Tea?" she repeated and glanced up at Trip.

"He drinks tea." His smile didn't waver. "But you wouldn't know that. I can't believe you've never met the guy."

"Not in person, no."

"You are a strange girl."

Aya glared up at him and again tried to step back. She had to get out of here. She had to think and to consider. How could she trust a guy who would make jokes at a time like this?

Fingers still linked behind her neck, he lifted his other hand to his chin and swiped over his stubble. His eyes tossed heavenward. "So as I understand it, you run around the country, trying to avoid detection from..." He glanced over his shoulder. "Those guys, whoever they are, writing songs to send to bands. You have how many Grammys?" He returned his stare to hers.

She shrugged and tried to turn away.

"No." Trip's voice firmed. "Wait. Listen to me."

"Why? I can't stay." She sighed. "You see what my life is like." She pointed to the building where a couple of plainclothes officers strode down the stairs. "I have no choice."

"Sure, you do. Choose me."

"Why?"

Tears brimmed his eyes, darkening the green. "Because I choose you."

Chapter Twenty

Aya hadn't been to a live concert in years. Yet here she stood to the side of the stage, flanked by Arnold and Maury. Out in the open. A shiver coursed down her spine. Any moment now, she'd wake from the dream of the last month.

She squinted up at Maury, and he smiled back. Warmth and affection radiated off him, and she tried to soak it into the chill of her bones. "'Bout time we got to know each other in person, eh?"

The cultured voice disrupted by the addition of the accented "eh" made her grin in return. "Yes." She nodded and glanced out into the audience. The crowd seethed with anticipation, an ocean humming in expectation, waiting for Trip's inaugural return to the music world as a solo act. Shouts and catcalls stood out amongst the general buzz of excitement.

Just within the circle of stage lighting, Aya spotted the dark-suited agents. The nemesis of her universe. Had she really escaped their influence?

"Relax," Maury leaned down to whisper in her ear. "Everything's fine."

Arnold jutted his chin in the direction of the agents, his moustache seeming to bristle. "Remember," he added as if reading her mind, "it's all in who you know." His bushy brows rose, and his finger flicked the side of his nose.

Aya shook her head. How could she believe it was true?

Yet here she stood.

A hand touched her shoulder, and she turned. Tears brimming eyes so much like her twin's, Evangeline embraced her, held her close, and kissed her cheek. "You made this night happen," she said, pulling back to smile. "You." She poked a finger at Aya's chest.

Emotion clogged her throat. In Eva, she'd found a sister, and through her, now discovered an extended family she never believed possible. Wendee, who had organized the concert. Maury, like a father she'd never known, stepped in and systematically took care of the legal side of her life, setting her free. She didn't have to hide anymore. He'd told her she didn't have to run, and at long last, she believed it to be true.

"No." Aya managed to form the word with effort over the tightness of her larynx. "You..." She swung her arm to encompass everything around her. "And—"

"Listen to me," Evangeline persisted, shaking her shoulders slightly. "Like a lifeline, you—you—brought him from the brink. You gave him new life. You returned my brother to me, a son to his mother, and a grandson to his grandmother. Whatever we did was small payment. We love you. I love you."

The tears flowed freely down Aya's face, a mirror to Eva's glistening cheeks. Neither tried to swipe them away. Again, they hugged tightly, like new-found sisters. Aya felt the beating of Eva's heart.

"Hey, hey," Arnold cut in. "Enough of that now. Let's see how the poor fellow does first. Might be the total shits, and we're all out of work."

Aya broke away and batted Arnold on the upper

arm. "He's gonna blow the ships outta the water tonight." She laughed, turning to see the many boats at anchor, their merry lights adding to the ambiance.

"That's right," Eva said. "He's got the voice, thanks to Grandma. He's got the location, thanks to family connections. He's got the songs, thanks to our girl here—"

"Don't forget the manager," Arnold cut in.

"And the lawyer," Maury added.

Aya noticed how Maury's gaze found Eva and how her new sister's color rose.

"Puh, on the lawyers," Arnold said. "No one ever thanks the lawyers."

"Now, that's true," Maury agreed with a clap of his hands.

They all chuckled.

Then the lights dimmed.

A general hush befell the crowd. Still the occasional shout and piercing whistle broke over the mob like a ripple. The ocean swayed in the background, setting the mood, and the iconic Hotel del Coronado sat majestically in the distance. Now, the full moon glowed down from its zenith like a spotlight, illuminating the grand piano sitting in the middle of the dais. The *Iron Clad* band members waited in the rear, and then the man himself seemed to just appear on stage.

He commanded the complete attention of everyone present, appearing to grow to enormous proportions. In a single drawn breath, the audience inhaled then erupted. Trip's wide grin consumed his face, and his eyes danced. In his element, he strode from one side to the other, waving and allowing the crowd to welcome him and enfold him into their affection. Then he stood to the middle again, approached the piano with a perceived reverence, and sat.

He glanced first at the keys then to the crowd, and twisting, he gazed at Aya. Their eyes met and locked, like a lover's embrace. A shiver sliced down her spine. A tingle replaced the previous cold, and warmth flooded in all the right places.

His attention returned to the instrument, then to the crowd. Trip's hands hovered above the keys, then one finger dipped. The first note hung in the air, and he leaned in to the mic. "I've new songs for a new version of me. I hope you like them."

"We love you, Trip," a woman screamed, and others echoed.

A bra landed on the stage.

Aya smothered a giggle.

Trip arched his head and laughed, the sound genuine and heartfelt. In his element, he moved so his lips returned to the mic. "I love you, too," he replied, staring into the sea of faces.

And then he began.

Aya's song, written for him, flowed from Trip as she had only imagined it would. Every note echoed a pulse to her heart. She hugged her arms around her middle, remembering the first time she'd taken a chance to hear Trip sing. She shook her head and stared up at the stars puncturing through the black void of the sky. Then she let her emotions flood and laughed aloud. "All for a song."

"What's that?" Maury looked down at her.

She swung her hand, taking in everything from the ocean, to the people, the heavens, and finally Trip, whose band, *Iron Clad*, had just stepped into the spotlight right on cue. "My song. Our work."

"Marvelous, isn't it?" He squeezed her shoulders, then tugged her to his side.

The melody floated, and then the final lines.

"When someone knows all of you,

When they know all you do,

All you've done, the good and bad,

And see beyond and are never sad…"

The words soothed like a balm, her song having a new life in the hands of the artist.

"When they love for who you are,

Now the stars just aren't that far."

Her song written for him, now his song being sung for her.

He stood amidst the applause and started toward her. Reaching for her hand, he swept her with him to center stage, and hugged her close. His lips found hers.

"I love you…for you."

A word about the author...

Let's face it...Lori likes tea. Most often found in the kitchen sharing stories, or a coffee shop, mug in hand, she can visit for hours.

That's inspiration: people, places, adventure. Every day is made up of the moments to create the tapestry of life.

Lori's body of work is as varied as the adventures of daily life and includes children's stories, a Gluten-Free cookbook, romance, suspense, and thrillers, and soon, Young Adult fiction.

Collaboration is important to improving one's craft, and as such, Lori is an active member of the TransCanada Romance Writers, Romance Writers of America, The Calgary chapter of the Romance Writers, The Alberta Romance Writers Association, and belongs to both a Critiquing group and a Beta Reading weekly group.

In all things, remember...life is a journey, thanks for being part of the adventure!

~*~

Find Lori online at:
http://www.loripowerwriter.com

Thank you for purchasing
this publication of The Wild Rose Press, Inc.

For questions or more information
contact us at
info@thewildrosepress.com.

The Wild Rose Press, Inc.
www.thewildrosepress.com

To visit with authors of
The Wild Rose Press, Inc.
join our yahoo loop at
http://groups.yahoo.com/group/thewildrosepress/